FROM THE
NANCY DREW FILES

THE CASE: Track down the kidnappers of Hal Colson, teenaged heir to a vast fortune.

CONTACT: Lance Colson, Hal's young and very handsome uncle. He manages the family estate but can't control his nephew's rebellious streak.

SUSPECTS: Monica Sloane, Lance's girlfriend. She can't conceal her dislike of Hal and his lifestyle.

Amy Tyler, Hal's explosive girlfriend. She seems bent on accusing everyone—except her own gang.

Mohawk and Goliath—two semi-toughs working their way up to full-fledged delinquency.

COMPLICATIONS: Two vicious attempts on Nancy's life—including a car bomb that totals Lance's expensive Maserati—convince the young detective that a killer is on her case.

Books in THE NANCY DREW FILES™ Series

Available from ARCHWAY paperbacks

THE NANCY DREW FILES CASE · 12

FATAL RANSOM

Carolyn Keene

AN ARCHWAY PAPERBACK
Published by POCKET BOOKS • NEW YORK

AN ARCHWAY PAPERBACK *Original*

An Archway Paperback published by
POCKET BOOKS, a division of Simon & Schuster, Inc.
1230 Avenue of the Americas, New York, N.Y. 10020

ISBN: 0-671-62644-2

First Archway Paperback printing June 1987

10 9 8 7 6 5 4 3 2 1

FATAL RANSOM

Chapter

One

"DAD, ARE YOU saying you don't want me to take this case?" Nancy Drew asked, her blue eyes locked on her father.

Carson Drew kept pacing back and forth in front of the sofa, where his daughter was sitting. "It's not that I don't want you to take it," he said.

"What is it, then?" Nancy asked, pressing her point.

"It's just that kidnappings are so dangerous. I've known of so many ugly incidents. . . ." Mr. Drew rubbed his forehead and stared past Nancy as though he were looking for the right words to express his feelings. "I wish I'd never told Lawrence Colson I'd talk to you about investigating this. *He* wondered if I should allow you to take the case. He said he wondered if it was too much for a girl your age to handle. Now I think he's right—especially when I'm going to be out of town for the next three weeks."

"I know the danger," Nancy answered emphatically, leaning forward. "I also know that a sixteen-year-old boy was kidnapped yesterday. If I don't make the right moves fast enough, that boy could die!"

"You could die, too," said her father. He stopped pacing and stood in front of her, looking down into her eyes. "I don't usually interfere with your cases, Nancy—"

"I won't make any wrong moves, Dad!" Nancy insisted. "You know I'm careful."

"All right," her father said after a second. "But I want you to promise me that you'll use your judgment—and if things get dangerous, you'll contact me."

Nancy smiled. "That much I can promise." Just then the doorbell rang and Nancy jumped off the sofa and went to answer it.

"We came right over," Bess Marvin said the instant Nancy opened the door.

"What's up?" George Fayne asked. "Sounds important."

"Come in and I'll tell you all about it," Nancy said, showing them into the living room.

"Hi, Mr. Drew," Bess said as she sat down. "Oh, Nancy, I forgot to tell you, we ordered a pizza for supper just before we came over. Double everything except anchovies. It should be delivered anytime now."

"That's my cue to get out of here," said Carson Drew. "You girls won't need any help from me! Nancy," he continued, *"if* you're going ahead with the case, you should have this. I was going to return it to Lawrence Colson, but if you're sure . . ."

It was a piece of folded paper. When Nancy opened it, two pictures carefully labeled Number One and Number Two fell out. She set them aside while she examined the letter. It was made up of words and letters cut from magazines and pasted onto high-quality bond paper.

"Today Hal looks like picture number one," the note said. Nancy glanced at the photo of a teenage boy who had been bound and gagged. His eyes were terror stricken. "We want $475, 000 by noon on Thursday, or Little Hal will be returned to you looking like photo number two."

Number two was an exact duplicate of the first picture—except for one thing. In the second photo, the boy's head had been removed.

"Do not contact the police," the note continued, "or you will never see him again. And remember, we're watching you." The last sentence simply said, "We'll be in touch."

No wonder her dad was apprehensive about the case! Nancy thought. "Thursday," she muttered. "This is Monday—less than three days. Sounds as though the kidnappers mean business. We have no time to lose."

She handed the note and pictures to her friends. George whistled. "These guys are intense!" she said.

"I don't want to think about it," said Bess. "Where's our pizza?"

"You're amazing, Bess," George said. "We're talking about a kidnapping and possible murder, and all you can do is wonder where the pizza is. Don't you ever think about anything besides food?"

"Yes," Nancy broke in. "Most of the time she thinks about boys."

"That's not fair," Bess argued.

George leaned against the arm of the sofa and glanced at Nancy. "It's weird that Bess and I can be cousins and be so different, isn't it?"

"What's really weird," Bess said, "is that we called for that pizza forty-five minutes ago and it's not here yet! I haven't eaten all day—nothing to speak of, I mean. I simply can't think about this case on an empty stomach."

Nancy was about to point out that that particular case might be even harder to think about on a full stomach, but she changed her mind. "I thought you were going to try to lose some weight, Bess," she said instead.

"I am. Tomorrow. I need to take off about five pounds—oh, there's the doorbell! Thank heaven!"

Nancy smiled to herself as she collected all their money and went to pay the delivery man. She wondered how many times Bess had lost those same five pounds.

No sooner was the pizza on the coffee table than Hannah Gruen appeared carrying a tray crowded with sodas, paper plates, and a mountain of napkins.

"I think she's on to us," George said as Hannah carefully put the tray down.

"Yes. I am." Hannah divided the napkins into three equal stacks and placed one in front of each girl. "You can't take care of a family for as many years as I have and not know that three girls eating pizza are going to make a mess."

Hannah Gruen had been with the Drews since Nancy's mother died, when Nancy was three. And I never really appreciate her until I'm about to start a dangerous case, Nancy thought to herself as she watched Hannah bustle around.

"Thanks, Hannah," she said. "For everything."

"Have fun, you three" was Hannah's answer as she left the room.

Bess pushed her long blond hair back behind her ears, scooped a piece of pizza from the box, and took two huge bites, one after the other. She sighed ecstatically and leaned back in her seat. "There. Now I can think about other things. So tell us the plan, Nan!"

"Yeah, Nancy," said George. "Fill us in."

Nancy settled into the corner of the sofa with a can of soda in her hand. "Well, the first move is for me to go over to Lawrence Colson's tonight and find out everything he knows so far. My dad said he's expecting me at eight."

"Lawrence Colson?" asked George. "Is he related to the Colson Enterprises people?"

"He *is* Colson Enterprises," Nancy replied. "He's one of my dad's clients. Colson called and told him about the kidnapping this morning. Dad said Mr. Colson was a nervous wreck."

"Who wouldn't be?" George said. "Think about what he's going through, worrying about his son."

"No, Hal is his nephew—not his son," Nancy said.

"And think about all that money! Even for a

man like Colson, parting with four hundred and seventy-five thousand dollars would be a problem," Bess added, reaching for another slice of pizza.

"Do the police know about this yet?" asked George.

"Colson didn't think it would be wise to get in touch with them yet—at least that's what my dad says," said Nancy. "He wants to find out more about the people he's dealing with. He's concerned that the threat in the letter is serious. He said he'd never forgive himself if he called the police and something terrible happened to Hal."

She stood up decisively. "I think I'll go change and get ready to see Mr. Colson."

"Okay, we'll clean up down here and walk out with you," said George.

The night air was warm and filled with the spring scent of honeysuckle. Nancy breathed in the fragrance and suddenly remembered sitting on the front porch with Ned Nickerson one evening a few weeks before, talking and gazing at the stars. She missed Ned. She wished he were there right then.

Nancy shook off the thought and climbed into her blue Mustang. She'd decided she shouldn't tell Ned about this case. He was busy writing a paper at school—Emerson College—and she didn't want him to be worrying about her. There would be plenty of time to fill him in later.

"Call us when you get home," George said as she and Bess walked to George's car.

Nancy waved an okay, pulled out of the driveway, and headed toward Allegheny Drive, the quickest route to Lawrence Colson's house.

She made her way along the winding road that led to the very posh residential area on the outskirts of River Heights. As darkness settled around her, Nancy brushed all thoughts of Ned out of her mind and started working on possible plans for rescuing Hal Colson.

Suddenly a car drove up behind her, its headlights shining straight into her rearview mirror. Nancy reached up and turned a switch on the mirror to eliminate the glare. But the car was following so closely that the entire rear window became filled with blinding white light. She increased her speed slightly—and the car behind her began going faster too. As she drove along, continuing to go a bit faster, the lights changed from a minor annoyance to a major problem.

"Why doesn't he just pass me?" Nancy muttered out loud as the two cars came to a long, straight stretch of road.

A few moments later the road started curving

again. Now it was too late for the other car to pass her. And it was moving up even closer.

Nancy felt a shiver of fear. The car had to be chasing her, and there was only one thing to do: outrun it. Nancy gunned the Mustang and took off like a shot—the phantom car staying with her.

Suddenly Nancy felt a jolt as the car tapped her back bumper. "He's trying to run me off the road!" she said out loud.

Nancy pushed the accelerator to the floor as she began to ascend a hill. She had to get away, but on the incline the Mustang didn't have enough power.

Then the phantom car made its move. The first jolt snapped Nancy's head backward against the seat. She gripped the steering wheel and fought to keep the Mustang on the road as the second jolt rocked the car.

The third blow came swiftly. Suddenly Nancy's car flew over the crest of the hill, careening out of control and straight into the path of an oncoming car.

Chapter

Two

NANCY GRIPPED THE steering wheel and held on for the full ride. Something her father had said a couple of years before flashed into her mind: "Never stop driving until the car comes to a complete stop." Good advice for a girl learning to drive. Better for a girl in a runaway Mustang.

Jerking the wheel to the left, Nancy sped by just in front of the oncoming car and landed in a clump of bushes on the left side of the road. The phantom car that had pushed her into that flight was nowhere to be seen, and the car she had almost hit didn't even bother to stop.

"Friendly folks," Nancy said, opening the car door and stepping out to check the damage.

The Mustang's back bumper was bent, but not too badly—certainly not badly enough to worry about right then. Nancy got back into the driver's seat and started the ignition.

It was only a few minutes after eight when she arrived at Lawrence Colson's house. *I was expecting a mansion,* she thought to herself, *but this is a palace!* A long, curving drive led up to a three-story brick house surrounded by formal gardens and magnificent oak trees. It looked like something belonging to a British aristocrat.

Nancy parked her Mustang in the drive beside a beautiful red Maserati. She wondered if it was Hal's. Lots of families out there could afford cars like that—but for a teenager? If it is Hal's, his uncle must be very generous, Nancy thought as she rang the doorbell.

A man who appeared to be in his midtwenties opened the door. For a second Nancy wished they had a person as good-looking as that to help Hannah. He was the handsomest butler she had ever seen—wavy brown hair, eyes so dark they almost looked black, and a tall, muscular build.

"I-I'm Nancy Drew," Nancy said. "Mr. Lawrence Colson is expecting me."

A smile spread across the man's somber face,

and a look of relief flooded his dark eyes. "I sure am! Come right in, Miss Drew."

"*You're* Lawrence Colson?" Nancy asked, following him inside. She'd been expecting someone much older.

"The one and only," he said. "But please call me Lance."

"Lance. Yes," Nancy managed to say, hiding her astonishment.

Lawrence Colson wasn't Nancy's only surprise. From her Mustang, she had tried to picture what the inside of his mansion would look like. She'd been totally off base on her guess about that, too.

Instead of the colonial pieces and huge fireplaces she had been expecting, contemporary furniture in white and beige filled the rooms. Thick, pale Oriental rugs covered the burnished wooden floors, and a couple of crystal chandeliers hanging from the ceilings added to the sophisticated look.

But the focal point of the house was the staircase that thrust its way up from the foyer into the second floor. It was breathtaking. For a minute Nancy imagined herself sweeping down those stairs in a flowing ballgown. . . .

"It is beautiful, isn't it?" Lance asked, interrupting her daydreams.

"Unbelievable," Nancy answered.

"This house belonged to my brother, Michael," said Lance. "He was the one who bought it and decorated it and loved it. I'm really just a live-in guest—and Hal's guardian, of course."

He shook his head. "Some guardian! It was bad enough that I couldn't keep him in school or away from those punk friends of his—but letting him get kidnapped? I'll never forgive myself. I'm not fit to be anyone's guardian." His eyes were anguished.

"I think you're being too hard on yourself, Mr. Colson," Nancy said gently and immediately corrected herself, "Lance." She ran her fingers through her reddish gold hair as she often did when she was trying to come up with the right words.

"I'm going to find your nephew." Nancy didn't add "dead or alive" because she didn't want to worry Lance even more. "I've got to work fast, though, and I need all the help you can give me."

"I'll do anything," Lance said simply. "Just tell me what to do. You are taking the case for sure?"

"Yes, I am taking the case. But we've got a lot to do. First, tell me everything you know about this kidnapping. Even the smallest detail may be helpful."

Lance escorted Nancy into the den, where she was seated on a white loveseat.

"I don't know much about it at all," he confessed. "When I came home from work last night I found a ransom note—the one I gave to your father. There was no sign of a break-in—but the door to my study had had the glass cut out, and the door had been unlocked and opened. The note was on my desk." Lance's eyes had a haunted, distant look, as if he were reliving the scene.

"Who would do something this horrible?" he asked her helplessly.

"That's what I'm going to find out. Now, when was the last time you saw Hal?"

Lance leaned back in his chair. "Yesterday. He said he was going to the Woodland Mall. That's the only place he's been spending his time lately." He frowned. "You know, I just haven't known how to handle Hal these days. I guess it's a good thing Michael isn't around to see how he's turned out. Michael wouldn't be able to take it if he knew that Hal's main goal in life is to be a roadie for a punk rock band. And that crowd he runs with—trash, all of them."

"Michael was—"

"Hal's father," Lance explained. "He's the one who started Colson Enterprises. When Michael and Karen, Hal's mother, were killed in a plane crash, their will stipulated that I would be Hal's guardian and that the running of the company was up to me until Hal turns twenty-five."

"When did they die?" Nancy asked.

"Two years ago in March."

Nancy knew that kids sometimes went off the deep end when their parents died. Maybe that was what had happened to Hal. But that wasn't the time to talk about it.

"Does anyone know Hal is missing?" she asked instead.

"No. Except you and your father."

Nancy couldn't help remembering the incident earlier out on Allegheny Drive. "I know this sounds crazy," she said, "but I was run off the road tonight on the way over here. I wonder if someone already knows I'm in on this case and would like to see me taken off it."

"Oh, no," Lance said immediately. "You weren't hurt, were you?"

"No. Just suspicious."

"I wouldn't be," Lance told her. "We've had trouble with teenagers running people off the road out here lately. The police are trying to catch the kids, but so far they haven't been successful. As a matter of fact, I was their target the other night." He grinned. "But my Maserati and I outran them."

So the Maserati is his, Nancy thought.

"Did you get a description of the car?" Lance asked.

"No. It was too dark. All I saw were the headlights."

"Too bad," Lance said. "But, as I said, I wouldn't worry about it. I'm sure it has nothing to do with Hal's disappearance."

He shook his head irritably. "The teens in this town are really getting out of hand. I read in the paper just this morning that the blood bank had reported several pouches of blood missing—blood, for God's sake!—and that they'd fired the teenager who'd been driving the delivery truck because they thought he'd taken it."

"Pretty strange. But not all River Heights teenagers are bad. I know that for a fact—I'm eighteen myself. But to get back to the kidnapping," Nancy reminded him, "do you have a photo of Hal?"

Lance was just about to answer when a tall, slender, dark-haired woman came into the room. She was wearing tailored pale gray pants and a matching sweater. Her beautiful face was bored and petulant looking.

"Hello, Monica," Lance said, getting to his feet. "Nancy, this is Monica Sloane. Monica, Nancy Drew. She's here to help us find Hal."

Us? Nancy thought. Monica wasn't married

to Lance. Nancy just smiled politely and nodded at the other woman.

Monica just stared at her. "So you're here to help Lance find little Hal," she said at last. Her tone was icy.

"Yes, I am," Nancy answered. "Do you know anything about this case that might help me?"

"No, I don't, Ms. Drew," snapped Monica. "And I couldn't care less about that stupid kid."

"Monica!" Lance protested. "This is no time—"

"She might as well know what I think," Monica said. "She'll probably try to ask me questions anyway."

"You're right," Nancy said cheerfully. "Why don't you tell me what you have to say now, Ms. Sloane? It might save both of us a lot of time and trouble."

Monica glared at her. "All I've got to say is this: it's just one more thing that crazy kid has done to mess everything up for Lance. Poor Lance is losing his shirt on his new project, and now he's going to have to pay ransom for that no-good brat who's part of the problem at the mall!"

Lance's face was crimson. "Monica, please. Try to control yourself. Nancy doesn't want to hear this."

But Lance was wrong. Nancy did want to hear it.

"What do you mean he's part of the problem at the mall?" Nancy asked.

"Do you know the new Woodland Mall?" Lance asked. Nancy nodded. "Then you know that we're having trouble renting some of the shops, and most people think that it's because of the punks that are hanging out there. And Hal *does* hang out there . . ."

"I see. Well, will there be a problem coming up with the ransom money—if we have to go that far?" she asked.

Lance shook his head. "No. As I said, we are having trouble with the mall project, but Colson Enterprises is still sound. And I think things will turn around once the mall is fully leased. That's the only problem right now."

"No, our problem right now is that kid and the kids he hangs out with," said Monica. "We didn't *have* problems until he started acting up."

Lance gave Monica a disapproving look. "Don't you have something to take care of upstairs?" he asked.

Monica's eyes swept Nancy's face coldly. "Yes," she said thoughtfully. "I think I do."

"I'm sorry," Lance said once she had left the room. "Monica and Hal have never gotten along.

"I have to admit, all this guardian stuff came as a big shock to me," he went on. "I had my own construction business before my brother died. It was small, but I was doing pretty well. I had to sell my business so I could devote all my time to Colson Enterprises. You know—keep the business running so Hal would have something to take over one of these days."

"That must have been a real sacrifice—especially when you had to start a new life so suddenly," Nancy said. She was starting to admire Lance Colson more and more.

"Monica and I used to have time for each other. But since I moved in here and took over Colson Enterprises—well, I just haven't had much time to be with her. I guess I'm not the greatest company these days, and she resents it."

"Resents" would be putting it mildly, Nancy thought, still a little chilled by Monica's parting glance. But all she said was, "I think I understand."

She stood up. "If you could provide me with a good photograph of Hal, I can get out of your way and get started solving this case."

Lance picked up a small photo from a table next to the den entrance. "I thought you might want this, so I had it ready for you."

"Someone who thinks like a detective," Nancy said, smiling. "We're going to make a great team. One more thing," she added as she started walking to the front door, "what kind of car does Hal drive?"

"A new white Mercedes convertible."

Nancy jotted it down in the little notebook she always took with her. "What's the license plate number?"

"HAL," Lance answered.

"That should be easy enough," Nancy said. "I'll get right on it."

She reached for the door handle, but Lance got there before her. "I really appreciate your help on this, Nancy," he said warmly.

. He opened the door—and then froze.

He and Nancy were face-to-face with a teenage girl. She had orange spiked hair on the left side of her head and shoulder-length purple hair on the right. And she looked furious.

The girl stared past Nancy at Lance. Finally she snarled, "Okay, Lance. What did you do with Hal?"

Chapter

Three

"WHAT ARE YOU doing here, Amy?" Lance asked angrily. "I thought I'd made it clear that I didn't want you around here anymore."

"It'll take more than *you* to keep me away from Hal," the girl answered. Her voice was strong and controlled. "I know you've done something with him. And I'm going to find out what—one way or another."

Lance's eyes were locked on the girl. His hands were trembling. He took a slight step forward. For a moment Nancy thought he was actually going to hurt Amy.

"Oh, give it a rest, Amy," he said at last. It

sounded as though he was forcing himself to be casual. "Your precious Hal has gone to his grandmother's up in Michigan."

"He didn't tell me that," Amy shot back.

"Maybe that's because he's not as crazy about you as you think he is. Could that be possible, do you suppose?"

"You wish!" Amy looked at Lance suspiciously. "Why would he decide all of a sudden to go visiting?" she asked. "That just doesn't sound like Hal to me."

Nancy could feel the pressure building. Poor Lance! she thought. He was having a hard enough time coping with Hal's disappearance, and this must seem like the last straw to him. Nancy decided to help him out a little.

"Hal went to his grandmother's because she's very sick," she said, deliberately moving closer to Lance to provide a united front against Amy. "We don't know when he'll be back. Probably next week some time."

"Who asked you?" Amy asked coolly, staring straight into Nancy's eyes. "Who *are* you anyway?"

"She's a friend of Monica's," Lance said. "If it's any of your business. Which it is not." He grabbed the doorknob and started to close the door. "Go away, Amy. This conversation is over."

But Amy jammed her foot in the doorway.

"I'll go," she said. "But you'd better have Hal call me as soon as he gets back. Understand?"

"Sure," Lance said. "Goodbye." He gently nudged Amy out of the way and closed the door. Amy kicked the closed door once, and then the room fell silent.

"What was *that* all about?" Nancy asked. "Who was that girl?"

"Amy Tyler," Lance said through clenched teeth. "Unfortunately, she's Hal's girlfriend. It seems they can't live without each other. She put on quite a performance, didn't she?"

"Performance? What do you mean?" Nancy asked.

Lance began pacing back and forth. "Oh, I don't know. Somehow I just can't believe she's that cut up about Hal being gone. If my hunch is correct, the only thing she's missing right now is Hal's money. Not Hal."

Nancy's mind was racing. The last time Lance had seen Hal, Hal had been on his way to the mall, where he usually hung out with his friends. Friends like Amy, who loved money? Was something starting to click?

"Do you think there's any possibility that Amy Tyler could be involved with this kidnapping?" Nancy asked.

"It wouldn't surprise me," Lance said. "I know she only hangs around Hal for his money —or his future inheritance. She probably

23

wouldn't mind trading him for the ransom." All of a sudden he sounded exhausted.

Nancy rested her hand on his arm for a second. "I've got to go," she said. "But I'll be back in touch tomorrow. Try to take it easy, okay?"

Lance nodded.

Nancy walked to the door again and then paused. "This is going to be all right," she said reassuringly. "I'm going to the mall first thing in the morning to see if I can come up with any clues."

"Keep an eye out for Amy," Lance said.

"I will. Is there anything else you can think of that I need to know?"

Lance shook his head. "I wish there were."

As Nancy reached out for the doorknob, though, Lance stopped her. "Wait. There is something. At the mall, get in touch with Lester Mathers. He's the head security guard there and an old friend of Michael's and Karen's. He might be able to tell you something about Hal."

"Will do."

The first thing Nancy did when she got home was to call Bess and George and fill them in on the case. The mall was so large that she knew she'd need help to investigate it the next day. Both of them agreed to help her, and they decided to meet in front of the glass elevator at whatever time Nancy decided.

She had just hung up the phone from talking to George when it rang again.

"Hi, gorgeous," came Ned's voice over the phone. "How are you doing? I'm sorry to call so late, but I got to missing you so much I just had to."

"Ned! No, it's—it's not too late. But what about your term paper? Shouldn't you be writing it instead of talking to me?"

Ned laughed. "Well, you know what they say about all work and no play. I think it's all right to take one break every twenty-four hours. Anyway, it's coming along okay."

"Umm . . . That's great," Nancy said. Her thoughts were running in a dozen different directions at once. She couldn't tell Ned about the case—and yet the case was really the only thing she could think about. How could she sound convincingly normal?

"Hey, are you all right?" Ned asked. "You seem a little preoccupied."

"No—no, not at all! I'm fine. Just a little tired, I guess."

"Why? Is a new case taking up too much of your time?"

"A new case?" Nancy tried to laugh casually. "Why do you ask?"

"Well," said Ned cautiously, "you have that slightly distracted tone that means a new case."

"Oh, Ned, it's nothing like that. I miss you, too, by the way." At least *that* was true, Nancy thought miserably. She didn't trust herself to talk to him any more. "Hey, why don't you give me a call when your paper's done, and we'll try to figure out a way to celebrate long-distance?"

"Well, okay," Ned said. Was he disappointed? It was impossible to tell. "Take it easy, Nancy. I love you."

"I love you too," Nancy whispered. "Goodbye, Ned."

Then she felt terrible. Had Ned thought she sounded cold? She knew that if she'd stayed on the line for one more minute, she would have told him everything. But she couldn't allow herself to think about Ned then. For the moment the only thing she could concentrate on was getting Hal back. And the best way to do that would be to get a good night's sleep so she'd be able to work the next day. But it was a long time before she fell asleep.

Nancy prided herself on being ready for anything at anytime. But she wasn't ready for her next phone call—the one that woke her early the next morning. "Hello," she said sleepily. She glanced at the clock. Six-thirty, an hour before she'd planned to get up.

"Nancy, it's Lance. We've found Hal's car. Someone must have driven it onto the property in the night. It looks pretty bad. Do you think you could get over here right away?"

"Be there in half an hour," Nancy said, and suddenly she was very much awake.

When Nancy arrived at the Colson mansion, she saw the white Mercedes convertible parked at the end of the long drive. The top was down, and the white interior was splotched with something.

Nancy jumped out of her Mustang and raced to the Mercedes. The dark reddish brown stains that covered the car's interior were all too familiar to her. It was horrifying to think about what might have put the car in that condition.

"It's blood, isn't it?" Lance said over her shoulder. He had just come out of the house.

"I think so, Lance," Nancy said. And the amount that's in the car isn't a good sign, she thought to herself. For the first time she was beginning to wonder if Hal was still alive.

She shook the thought out of her head and began to search the car for clues. There wasn't much there, except for a paper Halloween skeleton that hung from the rearview mirror.

"Is this usually here?" she asked.

Lance shook his head. "I've never noticed it before."

Carefully Nancy detached it from the mirror. A piece of folded notebook paper was taped to the back of the skeleton's chest.

It was another note. Magazine letters had been cut out to form the words that spilled across the page. "Waiting is not our game," the note said. "You have forty-eight hours to get the money—until 12:00 noon on Thursday. We will tell you where to drop it that morning." Under the message was a crude drawing of a vampire.

Silently Nancy showed the note to Lance. "What do you think?" he asked her after he'd read it.

"I think Hal's still alive," Nancy said. "And I think we'd better get the money ready. I was hoping not to have to take that step, but—"

She broke off and stared into the car again, hoping to find any other clue—a matchbook, a club pin, anything that might offer more than they had. But there was nothing. Except for the bloodstains, the car was clean.

Nancy glanced at the drawing on the note. "The paper and the quality of that drawing make me think we're dealing with amateurs," she said, more to herself than to Lance.

"You might be right," he answered. "I hope you are. Amateurs will be easier to catch, won't they?"

"Not necessarily," Nancy said. "I don't want to destroy your hopes, but if they are amateurs, their inexperience will make them more unpredictable and possibly harder to track."

And more dangerous, she thought to herself. Uneasily she remembered her father's warning. She knew then that she was going to have to be even more careful on the case. Nancy glanced at her watch. Time was running out.

"I had planned to have my two associates meet me at the mall this morning to check things out, but I need to change my plans," Nancy said. She glanced at Lance and then back at the car. "I'm going to have my friend Bess come over and get samples of these stains. She has a friend who can type the blood for us. Once we have that information, we'll be a little better off than we are now."

"Fine," Lance said. "Come with me. We've got a dozen or so phones in the house. You can have your pick to call her."

Nancy followed him into the mansion.

"There's a phone here in the foyer," Lance said, nodding to the one just behind the staircase. "But you'll have more privacy if you use the one in the library at the top of the stairs."

"Thanks, I think I will," Nancy said. Even though she had told Lance her plan, she didn't want him or anyone else to hear her conversation. The situation was more serious than she had led Lance to believe, and she needed to explain everything fully to Bess.

Nancy hurried up the stairs, her mind racing. But just as she cleared the top step, something jarred her off balance. Suddenly she was tumbling backward—and then before she knew it, she was falling down the stairs.

Chapter
Four

WHEN NANCY FINALLY did stop her fall, she didn't know which hurt more—her pride or her body. She sat at the foot of the stairs, pushed her hair out of her eyes, and tried to regain her composure.

"Are you all right?" Lance asked frantically, bending over to help her up.

"I will be." Nancy put her left hand in Lance's and tried to push herself off the floor with her right. There was a wrenching pain in her right wrist. "Ouch!" she cried, falling back against the wall.

"You're hurt!" said Lance.

Behind Nancy, Monica came delicately downstairs. She paused for a second when she saw the scene at the foot of the stairs.

"Call an ambulance right away!" Lance ordered her.

"No. Don't," Nancy said quickly. "I'll be all right." She struggled again to get to her feet, and this time she was successful. "I've probably just sprained my wrist a little."

"I still think you should see a doctor," said Lance.

Nancy ignored him. "Why did you push me down those stairs, Monica?" she asked, turning to face her.

"Monica!" Lance gasped.

"I didn't push her." Monica gave a sigh of exaggerated boredom. "She startled me. I was walking down the hallway, and she banged into me when she came charging up the stairs." She glared at Nancy. "How was I supposed to know that hiring a private detective would just mean having another kid around the house?"

Nancy's temper was simmering—but she forced herself to calm down. Although she didn't believe a word of Monica's story, she knew that getting angry would only give Monica the advantage. She took a deep breath instead and tried to will her arm to stop throbbing.

Lance stepped to her side. "I really do think you should see a doctor," he said, taking her good arm protectively. "Come with me. I'm driving you to the emergency room at the hospital."

"I don't need a *hospital*, Lance!" Nancy protested. "All I need is to get back to work!"

"This is my house, you're working for me, and you were injured as a result of something my guest did," Lance said. Nancy thought she could see a flicker of rage in Monica's eyes at the phrase "my guest." "We're going," Lance finished. "Now."

"Okay," Nancy said reluctantly. "But let's not take too much time. Your nephew is the important one here. Oh, I really have to call my friend Bess about that blood typing before we leave."

Before going upstairs Nancy turned back and fixed her gaze on Monica. "You'll be in charge while we're gone," she said. "If the kidnappers call, listen carefully to what they say and take down any message they leave for us. And, please, don't give anything away." Monica glared, but Nancy felt sure she'd gotten the message.

It was almost afternoon by the time Nancy and Lance got out of the hospital. The doctor had told her she'd be back to normal in a day or two.

"I've never understood why emergency rooms take so long," Nancy said. "More than two hours to tell me I have a sprain—which I already knew!"

Lance walked her to his car. "I'm just glad you weren't hurt worse than you are." His pace was slow, and Nancy thought she detected some kind of hesitation in his voice.

"I guess I'll take you back to the house so you can get your car, and then I'll go to the police. Maybe they can find Hal." He paused, then whispered, "Before it's too late."

Nancy stopped in her tracks. "Does this mean you're firing me?"

Lance dropped her arm and stepped back a pace. "No. I'm not firing you. I would never do that! But you've been injured. I can't ask you to stay on the case now!"

"Lance," Nancy said, "when I sign up for a case, I sign up for the duration. A little sprain isn't going to interfere with my work, believe me. I've been hurt worse than this lots of times! It's all part of the job. I still think I can get Hal back. You can call in the police if you want, but I'd still like to continue working. A sprained arm won't affect my brain. It won't even affect my physical ability that much."

"Nancy Drew," Lance said, "I take it back. If you want to stay on this case, I'm all for it. And I won't call in the police *yet*—in case the kidnappers meant it when they said they'd kill Hal if I did." He started for the car again, and then gave Nancy's left arm a gentle squeeze. "I don't think I've ever met anyone as dedicated as you. I wish Monica were more like you."

Nancy didn't answer. She was thinking that the only thing she had in common with Monica was that they were both female.

"I wish she had some direction in her life," Lance said. "It's so hard to get her to think about anything besides herself. If Monica were half as dedicated to something as you are to your work, she'd be—well, she'd be—"

Nancy cleared her throat. "I'm sure Monica must have some good qualities," she said, wondering what they might be.

Lance held the car door open for her, then went around to the driver's side and got in. For a minute he sat staring out the windshield at the crowded parking lot. "We used to care for each other," he said. "But not anymore."

Nancy wasn't sure what to say. "Things change," she finally ventured.

"Before the kidnapping we had finally decided to break up. It was hard on both of us. Harder on her, really, I suppose. That's why I told her she could stay at the house until she found a suitable place. Of course I'll pay for her new place until she gets a job. She'll probably choose the most expensive apartment she can find—but at the moment it seems worth the price."

That explained Monica's presence—and her attitude, Nancy thought to herself.

As they pulled out of the parking lot, Nancy told Lance what she thought he'd like to hear: "I'm sure everything will work out."

It wasn't what she believed.

It was afternoon before Nancy was able to investigate the mall, as she had planned to do in the morning. She and George walked together, hoping to find anything that they could use as a clue.

"I never come over here to shop, but I see what Lance meant," Nancy said. "This mall *is* a hangout for a lot of punk kids."

"There's nothing wrong with punkers," George said. "They're just kids trying to make a different kind of statement."

"I know," said Nancy, "but I am going to follow my lead on Hal's crowd until I know definitely if they're involved with this case or not."

"But just because they dress differently from us doesn't make them kidnappers!"

"You're right," Nancy said. "But Lance thinks Hal's girlfriend, Amy, knows something about all this. And the last time Lance talked to Hal, Hal said he was going to the mall. I just feel there has to be a tie-in here somewhere."

As they finished their round of the mall, Nancy added, "Lance gave me a security guard's name. I think I'll go see if he's on duty and check things out with him. Why don't you go ahead and make another round while I'm gone? Keep your eye out for anyone who looks like Hal Colson or Amy Tyler."

"Love to, Nancy," George said. "How will I recognize them?"

Nancy showed her the photo of Hal Colson. "This is Hal. All I can tell you about Amy Tyler is that she wears punk clothes and she has weird hair. Orange spiked on the left side, shoulder-length purple on the right. Shouldn't be too hard to find, actually—even in this crowd. Meet you back here."

"I'll do my best," George said.

They parted company, and Nancy turned off the main mall corridor and started down a hall with a sign that said Security. She walked a few feet down the short, narrow, isolated passageway, going by a couple of storerooms on the way.

The door marked Woodland Mall Security was ajar. Nancy raised her hand to knock, and at that moment she heard a female voice. "Soon this will all be over, and you'll be a rich man."

The voice was hauntingly familiar. But whose was it? And where was it coming from?

Nancy stepped closer and tried to peek through the crack in the open door.

Suddenly she heard a scuffling noise coming from the main mall corridor. She stepped away from the door to listen.

"Oh, no!" a woman screamed. "She's dead!"

Chapter

Five

NANCY RACED OUT into the mall corridor. What on earth was going on?

Once she was out in the open area, she saw a crowd gathered in front of a store across the way. She hurried over and wove her way into its center.

"What's happened?" she asked.

A young pregnant woman was lying on the floor. She opened her eyes, then looked up at Nancy and the crowd in total shock. "Oh," she murmured. "I—I must have fainted. I'm so sorry."

She tried to get to her feet, but only succeeded in raising herself to a sitting position. The people crowding around her began to disappear one by one, apparently disappointed that something more dramatic hadn't happened.

Nancy grimaced. That's crowd mentality for you, she thought. "Are you hurt? Is there anything I can do to help you?" she asked the woman.

"You could help me up," she said, and laughed.

Nancy did. Once the woman was on her feet again, Nancy asked, "Can I get you to a doctor?"

The woman grinned. "No. I'll be fine now. This happens to me all the time." She thanked Nancy and walked away.

Nancy watched for a few seconds to make sure the woman stayed on her feet. Then she looked around to see if George had been in on any of the excitement. There was no sign of her—but who was that disappearing into that expensive shoestore down the corridor? It looked like Monica! Nancy ran down the hall and burst into the store.

"Where's the woman who just walked in here?" she asked the haughty-looking salesman who had immediately approached her.

"I'm sorry, miss, but you—" But Nancy had already spotted Monica in the corner, where she was trying on an expensive pair of green snakeskin boots.

"Monica!" Nancy exclaimed. "What are you doing here? Did anyone call for Lance while I was at the hospital? Were there any messages?"

Monica looked incredulous—and disgusted. "You followed me in here to question me?" she asked. "I didn't stick around after you left, if that's what you mean. I'm not your personal secretary."

"I asked you to stay by the phone," Nancy said angrily. "I'd have thought it was the least you could do, since you were the reason Lance had to take me to the hospital."

"Well, you'll just have to think again," Monica purred. "Get it into your head that I don't care anything about what's happened to Hal. All right?"

"But he's Lance's nephew! Don't you at least—"

"Could you come over here a minute?" Monica interrupted, raising her voice and beckoning to the salesman. In an instant he was at her side.

"This girl is really pestering me," she said. "Is it too much to ask that I be allowed to do my shopping in peace? You'd think the least you could do would be to keep people from loitering in here."

The salesman turned to Nancy. "I'm afraid I'll have to ask you to leave right away. You're upsetting one of our best customers," he said coldly.

"But I—" Nancy began.

"Go play detective somewhere else," said Monica.

"Please, miss. Before I call security," said the salesman.

Nancy left without a word. She couldn't trust herself to speak.

But at least the salesman had reminded her of where she had been heading originally. She walked back to the security office and approached the door slowly. This time, though, the door was closed, and there were no sounds coming from the other side.

Nancy knocked lightly, and a heavyset man in a gray uniform opened the door.

"Excuse me, could you tell me where I can find Mr. Mathers?" Nancy asked.

"That's me," the man said. "Can I help you?"

Nancy smiled. "I'm Susan Bigelow," she said. "From WBBB." She hoped Lester Mathers wasn't too familiar with the local TV newscasters. "We're doing a story about the new mall, and I thought you might be able to give me some information. Maybe a unique slant I could use to open this series. What kind of place is it to work at?"

She couldn't tell by his expression whether he was buying her story, but she was determined to stay with it.

"Well," he said, rubbing his forehead, "I have to say I can't imagine why anyone would want to watch a story on TV about this mall. What's there to say about it that isn't depressing? It's falling down around everyone's ears!"

"Falling down? What do you mean?" Nancy asked.

"I didn't mean it literally, of course. It's just that with all these kids hanging around here and everything—"

"The kids cause a problem?"

"Well, it's not anything you could put your finger on, exactly. It's just that there are so many of them, and they all look so weird. They fight a lot, and when they aren't fighting they just stand around and stare at people. Why'd they have to pick *this* mall? It's driving business away!"

"Do you know any of the kids personally? Do you ever talk to any of them?" asked Nancy. Maybe he'd end up helping her after all.

Lester Mathers laughed shortly. "They don't exactly drop in for tea, if that's what you mean. The only ones I know are the ones who cause trouble. Why, just a few days ago I—"

He broke off and stared strangely at Nancy.

"What kind of story did you say you were doing?"

"Just some sort of human interest thing," Nancy said evasively. She was dying to know what he'd been about to say, but she didn't want to make him suspicious. Instead she pulled out her picture of Hal and showed it to him. "Do you know this boy?"

Lester looked at it for a second. "Why, that's young Hal Colson." He shook his head. "Michael Colson's son. He sure don't take after his old man. Good thing Mike's not around to see him now."

"So you knew Michael Colson?"

"Yes, I did," said Lester quietly. "I thought the world of him too. Wonderful personality. When he was alive, this place was just getting started. Construction men all over, nothing finished—but he gave you the feeling that it was going to be the most beautiful set of shops in the world. And he knew each of us by name. He could really make you feel like a part of things."

He shook his head again. "Like I said, things have changed. It sure isn't the same kind of place now."

"I heard somewhere that the mall wasn't filling up quite as fast as Michael Colson must have expected," said Nancy.

"It's true. The new guy just doesn't have the

right touch, I guess. Look at all those empty storefronts! He hasn't rented out any new space in a long time. If they don't watch out, it'll be a ghost town around here."

"But Lance told me he thinks that's only temporary," Nancy said quickly.

"Lance? You mean you know Lawrence Colson?" Lester's expression was suddenly guarded.

"I—well, I talked to him before I started work on the story, of course," said Nancy. Inside she was furious with herself. She had wanted to defend Lance so much that she completely derailed the interview. Now Lester was rising to his feet, and he looked angry.

"What are you trying to do, Miss Bigelow?" he asked. "Get me in trouble? Make me spill the beans on the boss? Is that what you call 'human interest'—getting me fired?"

"No, no!" Nancy said. "I didn't mean to upset you. I only wanted a little background—"

"Sure you did! You reporters are all alike. Get out of my office."

"Mr. Mathers, I promise you, you're making a mistake," Nancy said, trying to sound calm. "If you'll only listen to me for a second—"

"I told you to leave. This is the only job I have, and I'd like to keep it. Now move! The interview is over."

Nancy stood up, and as she did she noticed a row of videotapes on a shelf over Lester's head. All of them were labeled Scanner. They must be security tapes of the mall—and perhaps Hal was on some of them!

Well, that wasn't the exact time to ask about them. "Goodbye, and thank you for your help," Nancy told Lester politely. "I hope you enjoy seeing the story on TV."

"Just get out of here" was his answer.

Out in the corridor again Nancy stood still, thinking. She had to get hold of those tapes, and as soon as possible. But what was the best way to do it?

"Nancy!" Bess and George were heading toward her. "I just caught up with George," said Bess breathlessly. "I wanted to tell you right away—my friend called me, and the blood type in the car was A negative. At least we have that much to go on."

She shook her blond hair back and rolled her eyes. "I'll tell you something else too. If this weren't such a life-and-death situation, I wouldn't care if this case never ended. That Lance Colson is a *hunk.*"

Nancy and George glanced quickly at each other, trying to conceal their smiles. Nancy knew they were thinking the same thing—Bess was in love again.

"How'd you make out with that security guard?" George asked.

Nancy shook her head. "I didn't. That is, I started out fine, but he clammed up when I mentioned Lance. I don't think he'll say anything more. But I've got to get back into his office. Let's go get something to eat while I think of a way to do it."

A chocolate shake apiece later, Nancy had come up with a plan. As the girls walked down the narrow corridor that led to the security office, she told Bess and George, "Remember, make it sound like a big deal."

She slipped into one of the storage rooms and listened as George and Bess went racing past her. Frantically they pounded on Lester Mathers's door.

"Help!" Bess shrieked. "Fight!"

He jerked open the door. "Where? What's going on?"

"There's a big fight down at the end of the mall! A whole bunch of kids. They're trashing the place!" Bess said.

"We came to get you as fast as we could," George added.

Nancy smiled to herself. She could always count on Bess and George to give great performances. They'd almost managed to convince *her* something was wrong.

"Come on!" said Bess. "We'll show you where it is."

Lester, Bess, and George dashed past Nancy's hiding place. Lester was hurriedly pulling out his walkie-talkie to speak to his guards.

"Fight!" he radioed. "B section. I'm on my way."

Quickly Nancy slipped around the corner and through the security office door, which had been left open by George. George had made sure she was the last one out, so the door hadn't been deadbolted.

Nancy darted to the rack of videotapes above Lester's desk. All of them were dated. Perfect, Nancy thought. She followed the dates until she found Sunday's tape—the tape of the day that Hal had vanished. "This might show us something," she murmured, slipping the tape into her oversize shoulder bag. She grabbed the tape from the previous Wednesday, too, just to have something to compare Sunday's tape to.

Carefully she rearranged the tapes in that section of the rack so Lester wouldn't notice that two were missing. Then she glanced around the office to see if there was anything else there that might be useful.

Nothing she could see. She was starting to get nervous because she didn't know how long Bess and George could keep Lester occupied. But she knew it was time to get out of there. Quietly she opened the office door.

"What do you think you're doing?" Lester Mathers said, looking her straight in the eye.

Chapter

Six

NANCY HAD BEEN right. It *had* been time to get out of there.

"Sorry to bother you again," she said. "I—I think I left something in here. My notebook. Have you seen it?"

Lester walked past her into his office. He sat down at his desk and leaned back in the creaky swivel chair, staring at the ceiling. "Now, why is it that I don't believe you?" he asked slowly.

"I know it was dumb of me," Nancy said with what she hoped was a convincing giggle.

"No, Miss Susan Bigelow, it was dumb of me," he answered. "You set up that fight, didn't you? So you could snoop around in here. What are you, some kind of spy for Colson?"

"No! Of course not! I had nothing to do with that fight! I'm just trying to do my job!" Nancy said. It's truer than you know, she thought.

"Well, don't come around here anymore, job or no job, or I'll see to it that you never set foot in this mall again." He stood up. "I'll walk you out," he finished grimly.

As she exited from his office, Nancy suddenly noticed a pay phone just outside the door. It made her remember the girl's voice she had overheard earlier. If only she'd had a chance to follow up on that!

Lester deposited her at the wide mall corridor.

"Thank you very much!" Nancy managed to say cheerfully as he stalked off. This time he didn't even bother to answer her.

"Three strikes and you're out," she muttered under her breath. Three times she had been kicked out in the mall—twice from Lester's office, and once from the shoestore. Perhaps she had been there long enough.

She could see Bess and George down the corridor, and Nancy headed toward them. On her way she passed a muscle-bound boy about sixteen years old. He was wearing oversize tennis shoes with no laces, baggy pants, and a studded leather jacket over a torn T-shirt. His head had been shaved, and he had three cross-shaped earrings in his right ear.

"Hey, Dracula!" a pink-haired girl called out as she passed by him. "Where've you been?"

"Hey, yourself!" he answered. "How's it going?"

"Dracula"? The note in Hal's car had had a picture of a vampire at the bottom. Could this kid possibly be connected with the note?

It was a long shot, but one worth following. Nancy motioned for Bess and George to follow her. Weaving her way through the crowd, she followed Dracula as fast as she could. But just as she was about to catch up with them, someone grabbed her arm and spun her around.

"What do you think you're doing?" a voice asked.

She was face-to-face with Amy Tyler.

"Look, you," Amy said. "I don't know why you were following him, but in the future, don't. Just leave him alone—if you know what's good for you."

Nancy took a deep breath. "And who appointed you guardian angel of Woodland Mall?" she asked.

"He's a friend of mine. Friends stick up for friends," Amy replied.

"Tell us about it," George said, moving up behind Nancy. Bess was next to her. But Amy didn't pay any attention to them. She was still glaring at Nancy.

"I think you'd better know something," she said. Her voice was almost a growl. "Any friend of Monica Sloane's is an enemy of mine. So stay out of my way."

Nancy burst out laughing. Amy sounded exactly like someone from an old, melodramatic movie. "I'll try to do that," she said. "Thanks for the warning, Amy."

Amy tried to answer, but she was so angry she was stuttering. Finally she turned and walked away.

"What was that all about?" asked George.

"That, boys and girls, was the one and only Amy Tyler," Nancy answered. "Hal Colson's girlfriend." She scanned the mall quickly. Dracula was nowhere to be seen. "And she's just spoiled the best lead I've had so far," she added with a sigh.

"Who's Monica Sloane?" Bess asked.

"She's Lance Colson's ex-girlfriend. She happens to be living in the Colson mansion right now, but I understand she'll be moving out as soon as she has a place of her own."

Bess's face had no expression. "Lance didn't mention her when I was over there," she said. "Why is that, do you think?"

"I guess she's not on his mind that much anymore," said Nancy.

Bess brightened. "Of course not! A guy who was as open and friendly as Lance was to me today can't possibly be attached to anyone. Probably he's forgotten all about her already. I can usually tell about stuff like that."

"I'd like to meet this open, friendly guy," George said.

"Actually, you're about to," Nancy said. "I was just thinking that we had pretty much exhausted the possibilities here. Let's go back to the Colson mansion and touch base with Lance."

"Great idea," said Bess. "Drive fast."

It was almost dinnertime as the three friends walked up the driveway toward the Colson house. Nancy noticed a piece of paper hanging out of the door of Lance's car. Another note? She opened the door and removed it; it was some kind of brochure.

"What's that?" asked Bess.

Nancy stared at the paper in the half light. A travel brochure," she said. "For Saint-Tropez." She stuffed the brochure into her bag. It was probably nothing, she thought, but the brochure did look brand-new. Why would Lance be thinking about traveling at a time like this?

After Nancy had introduced George to Lance, she briefed him on their afternoon and then asked him about his.

"Well, Monica did some errands—"

"Yes, I ran into her," Nancy said dryly.

"And I took a walk. I just needed some time to myself to clear my head and try to cope with all this. It's really starting to get to me."

"I can understand that," Nancy said warmly. "But, Lance, don't you think you should stay by the phone in case the kidnappers try to call?"

"I—I guess I forgot about that," said Lance.

"Of course!" Bess said, placing a protective hand on his arm. "You've been under a terrible strain. It's such a shame you can't get away from all this."

That reminded Nancy. She took the brochure out of her bag and showed it to him. "This was sticking out of your car door," she said. "I picked it up—I hope you don't mind."

Lance shrugged. "Saint-Tropez. I'd forgotten all about it."

"Who could forget Saint-Tropez?" George asked casually.

"Hal and I were planning to go on a vacation," Lance said. "I thought it might be a good idea to get away for a while, just the two of us." He laughed hollowly. "We actually thought we might be able to settle our petty differences if we were on neutral ground."

"Sounds like a great idea to me," Bess said. "If anything could do it, I bet that would."

Nancy wished Bess would slow down. When

she had a crush on someone, Bess went deaf, dumb, and blind. She supported her man at every turn. It was like being with a live country-and-western song.

But Bess's face fell when Lance mentioned Monica. "I'd appreciate it if you didn't tell her about these travel plans," he said. "She wasn't going to be included. And now that we aren't going to take the trip anyway, there's no point in upsetting her."

"Didn't you think she might have missed you?" Nancy asked.

"Well, yes," Lance said. "But actually, I thought she would be gone by the time we left. I expect her to be moving out any day now. Really." He glanced quickly at Bess.

The look in Bess's eyes was one of sheer delight. She moved a little closer to Lance, and her arm brushed against his.

"Have you ever been to Saint-Tropez?" Lance asked her.

Bess flushed. "No, but I'd love to go," she said with a giggle.

Subtle, Nancy thought to herself. Really subtle.

Lance was smiling. "Actually, Saint-Tropez was Hal's idea," he said. "I wanted to go to Monaco. But they're pretty close . . ."

Nancy couldn't quite tell why the casual flirtation between Lance and Bess was bothering her. Was it because she was missing Ned? Because she felt lonely—or left out? Because Bess was making a fool of herself? Or because it seemed so strange that Lance would even bother to put the moves on someone when his nephew was in such awful danger?

She tried to shake off her irritation. She knew that people in difficult situations often acted in ways that seemed inappropriate—just to ease the terrible fear they were dealing with. Lance was probably one of those people.

It's understandable for him to do this, Nancy told herself, watching Lance turn on the charm once again for Bess. She supposed she couldn't fault either one of them. But she still felt vaguely annoyed.

It was time to get back to reality. "Lance," she said decisively, "Lester Mathers didn't help me much. And somehow I don't think he'll want to talk to me any further. Is there anything else you can tell me about this case? Anything at all that might produce another lead?"

Lance thought for a minute. "No, nothing." He frowned, then added, "But I'm still sure that Amy has something to do with Hal's disappearance. As I said, she'd do anything for some of his money."

Nancy leaned forward. "I'm going to do everything I can to link Amy and that other kid, Dracula—if that's really his name—to Hal, but so far I don't have anything. It's true that Amy doesn't dress like Miss Teen America, but that doesn't mean she's guilty of anything."

Nancy patted the shoulder bag hanging on the arm of her chair. "I have two of the mall's scanner tapes. I—uh, borrowed them. They might produce something for us, but it's not likely.

"There *is* the blood in Hal's car," she added. "Bess's friend identified it as being A negative—"

"I wouldn't worry about that blood, Lance," Bess broke in. "You know how it is—when you get even a little cut on your finger, the blood gets all over everything before you can get it stopped."

But Lance didn't look as if he needed reassuring. He was smiling again.

"I've been worrying about that blood ever since we found the car," he said. "But, thank you, I'm not worried now. Hal's blood type isn't A negative. It's O positive."

Chapter

Seven

THAT NIGHT WAS one of the few times Nancy couldn't wait to get Bess out of her car.

"I still can't believe how gorgeous he is!" Bess kept saying all through dinner and even after they'd dropped George off. "Don't you think he likes me too? I mean, I know I'm younger than he is, but not that much. But, of course, this isn't the time to think about that—not with such a tragedy hanging over his head. Isn't it touching the way he's so concerned about Hal? He must really care a lot about people—"

She didn't even notice that Nancy wasn't paying attention or saying anything.

When Nancy dropped Bess off—still prattling on about Lance—she breathed a sigh of relief. Now she could start trying to think things through.

The problem was that none of the things she had learned so far fit together. There was the ransom note, the one Hal had found, printed on that expensive paper. Something about that note was bothering Nancy, but she couldn't put her finger on it.

Then there was Monica. Good old Monica. She obviously didn't care a thing about Hal. She blamed him for destroying her relationship with Lance. And from all outward indications, she was glad to have him out of the picture. But did she want Hal out of the way permanently?

There was Amy too. Where did Amy fit into all this? It was certainly strange the way she'd turned up at the mall at the exact time Nancy was there. Had she known Nancy would be there? And had she been the one Nancy had overheard telling someone he would be a rich man soon?

The blood-spattered car—spattered with someone else's blood. The notebook paper with the vampire sketch at the bottom.

And what about Lester Mathers, the head of security at the mall? He'd seemed perfectly willing to talk to her—*until* she'd mentioned Lance's name. Then he had clammed up. Did he know something about Lance, or did he, too, have something to hide?

Nancy shook her head as she pulled into her driveway. All she had were questions—and the longer she thought, the more questions she had. She knew that there was no point in trying to force answers to come. She would just have to wait—and let her subconscious get to work.

Maybe watching the scanner tapes from the mall would help. Nancy went into the house and inserted the Wednesday tape into the video recorder in the den and sat back on the sofa to watch.

Just then Hannah came in. She was already in her bathrobe, ready to relax for the evening. "Nancy," she said. "I didn't know where you were all day. Are you okay?"

"Just fine, Hannah. I didn't mean to make you worry. Sorry. I'm just going to watch this tape and then I'm going to bed early." She blew Hannah a kiss and turned back to the tape after Hannah had left.

It showed—well, a typical mall. Kids walking around. More kids. A mother yanking her toddler back into his stroller. Not much there.

Nancy's brain was ticking away as she watched. How did the kid called Dracula fit into the picture—if he *did* fit. And what about that Saint-Tropez travel brochure? It seemed strange that Lance would plan to take Hal on an

61

expensive vacation when he was supposed to be worried about money. Maybe Hal didn't know about his uncle's financial problems. Maybe there was some reason why Lance didn't want him to know about them!

Nancy watched the entire Wednesday tape without finding anything. She pulled it out and replaced it with Sunday's tape. "This one had better be good," she murmured. "I'm tired of striking out."

The tape started to roll. Nancy sat up with a start when she saw some kids who looked familiar—but then she fell back again. The reason they looked familiar was that she had just seen them on the other tape. Do they *live* there? she wondered. When do they ever go home?

All of a sudden she yawned. Her eyelids were growing heavy, and she stretched out on the couch with a throw pillow under her head. When she caught herself dozing, though, she forced herself to sit up again. And even though she was sleepy, she was still on the job.

Wait! Nancy literally jumped to her feet. Hal Colson was on the screen! She grabbed the remote control and rewound the tape until she found the place where he'd first come into view.

Her heart was racing. Yes, there he was. A perfect shot. He was even wearing the same clothes as he had been in the ransom picture—a faded denim jacket covered with buttons of rock stars, a black T-shirt, and black jeans. But his outfit couldn't disguise what was basically a clean-cut preppy face. Bess should meet *him*, Nancy thought to herself. He's even better looking than his uncle.

Hal was talking to two tough-looking kids. One of them was tall, thin, and wiry. He had a Mohawk haircut and was wearing a baggy shirt and baggy pleated pants with the legs rolled up to just below his knees.

The other guy was *huge*. He had two different haircuts—almost shaved on one side, and long and straight on the other. His face was stubbly with a day's beard, and he had a tattoo on one cheek.

As Nancy studied the tape more closely, she thought she remembered seeing those two boys in the other tape as well. Now they were whispering to Hal, who kept glancing over his shoulder. Was he looking for someone—or making sure they weren't overheard? It was hard to tell.

Then all three boys slapped hands together, laughed, and walked out of camera range.

Well, Hal certainly hadn't been in danger at that point. Nancy replayed the tape again and studied the periphery this time. She was hoping to catch a glimpse of Amy or Dracula, but they were nowhere to be seen.

It wasn't a lot to go on, but it would definitely do for then. At least she knew what some of Hal's friends looked like—and at least she had a *slightly* better idea of the time he'd been kidnapped. Nancy finally turned off the recorder and went to bed, deciding she'd return to the mall the next morning to try to find one or both of the boys who'd been talking to Hal. They might have been the last people to see him before he was kidnapped!

In bed Nancy ran everything through her mind one last time. She decided that she would never crack the case unless she could gain the confidence of a few of Hal's friends. They might be able to give her a clue—even a small one would be welcome right then. The case was going nowhere, and time was running out fast. She fell asleep, but then woke up a few hours later, still thinking about the case.

"I'll go undercover," she murmured to herself drowsily. It seemed like a great idea until she was fully awake. Then Nancy realized it wouldn't work. Amy and Dracula already knew her face.

Suddenly she had another—better—idea. She glanced at the digital clock on her bedside table. It was 2:20 A.M., but she didn't want to wait.

She picked up the phone and called George. "Mmmm-hello?" George said groggily.

"George. Nancy. I've just had a great idea, and you'll be perfect for it. You're going to go punk!"

"Nancy? Is that you?"

"Yes, it's me! Wake up, George! I saw Hal Colson on that scanner tape I got from Lester's office. He was talking to a couple of his friends, and I realized they'd probably be our best lead to Hal. But some of them would recognize me if I went undercover. So, will you do it? You'd be great!"

"Ummmmm—"

"Amy only saw you for a second when she was talking to me in the mall. With the right outfit you'd never be recognized. Come on, George! It'll be so easy!"

"Okay, Nancy, I'll do it," mumbled George. "Just let me get a little more sleep first."

"Sure. Sorry. Be here at eight in the morning, okay? Oh—and get Bess to fix you up before you come. She's good at that kind of thing."

"Eight?" George sounded a little more wide-awake now. "Why eight, Nancy? How early do you think those kids get up? *Some* people like to sleep late."

"Oh, all right. Nine-thirty, then," Nancy said. "Thanks, George."

"Yeah. Tomorrow. Bye." And George hung up.

She and Bess were at Nancy's promptly at nine-thirty the next morning. "You *are* perfect for this!" Nancy said as George walked into the den.

"Turn around and let her get the full effect," said Bess. "I really think this is my masterpiece, Nancy."

George did a pirouette in the center of the floor. The pink stripe Bess had sprayed through her hair provided an excellent camouflage. Combined with dead-white foundation and heavy eyeliner, the hair made George almost unrecognizable. She was wearing a black sleeveless sweatshirt, a black leather miniskirt, black fishnet stockings, black ankle-high boots, and about ten necklaces.

"No one will know who you are," Nancy said. "I can't even believe it's you. Great work, both of you!"

She played them the scanner tape twice. Then she announced, "Now for the plan."

"George, I want you to go over to the mall to see what you can find out. Do whatever you have to do to get close to some of those kids. But be careful—we don't know how, or if, they fit into this at all."

"Got it," said George.

"Bess," Nancy continued, "I want you to go to the mall too. Trail George at a distance. Don't let her out of your sight. If these kids *are* involved, it could be really dangerous. Call me if you notice anything out of the ordinary— anything.

"I'm going over to the Colson mansion to talk to Lance. Then I'll meet you both back at the mall."

Bess was pouting. "I have a much better idea. Why don't *you* go spy on George, Nancy? I'll take care of your business with Mr. Gorgeous."

Nancy flashed her a grin. "Nice try, Bess. But no go."

When Nancy arrived at the Colsons', she interrupted Lance as he was finishing his breakfast. Nancy knew that Lance hadn't gone to the office since the kidnapping on Sunday. Now it was Wednesday, and Nancy thought it was admirable of him to have dropped everything until he had some word about Hal.

"There's no news," Lance said as he walked into the foyer to greet Nancy and escort her into the living room.

"Well, I have some," she answered, telling him about what she'd seen on the scanner tape and the plan she'd put into motion that morning.

"Our time is running out, Lance," Nancy

said. "I know this is a long shot, but we have to do something."

"You're right," he agreed somberly.

Nancy paused for a second. She'd been thinking about something else on the drive over. "Lance, I don't want to alarm you," she said. "But I think you'd better go to the bank and get the ransom money today."

"What?"

"It's nothing to worry about," Nancy said. "But we could hear from the kidnappers at any time. Today's Wednesday, but they said we'd hear from them again by tomorrow morning. We may as well be ready. Once they make contact, there'll be no time to waste."

"I'll go right now," Lance said instantly. He looked thoughtful, then said, "Monica will be here this morning. She can man the telephone while I'm gone."

Nancy wasn't sure he was right. The last time Monica had been told to stay by the phones, she went shopping instead. But it would have to do. Nancy couldn't sit around the house waiting for Lance to get back—she needed to get to the mall.

Monica's reaction to Lance's plan was no surprise to Nancy. "I don't want to stay here and baby-sit a telephone!" she protested. "Who do you think I am?"

Lance grimaced. "Nancy, why don't you go

on ahead?" he asked. "I'll just—just finish things up in here."

Nancy guessed that he didn't want her to overhear an argument. She didn't want to stick around to hear it either. "Sure," she said. "I'll call you later."

She climbed into her car and turned the key. Nothing happened. Nancy tried again. Still nothing. What a time to have engine trouble! she thought.

Just then Lance stamped out of the front door. He looked furious, but he managed to compose himself when he saw Nancy. "What's up?" he asked.

"Engine trouble," she said disgustedly.

"Mind if I use your phone to call the auto club?"

"Be my guest," Lance said. "Uh—I wouldn't go upstairs if I were you. Monica's up there."

"I understand," Nancy said.

In a few minutes she'd rejoined him on the driveway. "Someone will be here in an hour," she said. "To either start the car or tow it away, or something. I'll just wait out here until they come."

"Get in," Lance said, pointing to his Maserati. "I'll drop you off at the mall on my way to the bank. It's almost on the way."

"Thanks, Lance," Nancy said gratefully.

Lance got in beside her, put the key in the ignition, and turned it. Then he slapped his forehead. "Wait a minute," he groaned. "Now *I've* got to go back inside. I forgot to get a briefcase to put all that money in."

Nancy smiled and shook her head as he disappeared into the house. The morning was really getting messed up. What else could possibly go wrong?

As if on cue, a car honked. Nancy turned around and saw Bess pull up and park farther down the driveway. Bess jumped out of her car and waved frantically at Nancy.

"What's she doing here?" Nancy said to herself. Something must have happened to George! Quickly she got out of Lance's car and ran toward Bess.

Suddenly there was an explosion behind her, and Nancy was hurled into the air.

Chapter
Eight

WHEN THE DUST settled, Nancy was face-down on the driveway, and the first thing she heard was Bess screaming, "Are you all right? Nancy? Are you all right?"

For a minute Nancy didn't move.

"Nancy!" Bess shrieked.

Nancy turned over and looked at the smoke rising from Lance's car. "I'm all right," she said, staggering to her feet. "If you hadn't pulled up and honked when you did, though, I wouldn't have been. Good timing, Bess!"

As Nancy walked toward the wreckage of the Maserati, Lance came rushing out of the house. His face was white.

"What happened?" he demanded. "I—I don't understand—"

"It's pretty clear," Nancy said matter-of-factly. "Somebody bombed your car."

"Somebody—my car—"

Lance looked as if he were going to be sick.

"Obviously these guys are not going to stop at kidnapping," Nancy said.

Bess finished the thought. "They're out for murder."

"But—but this doesn't make sense," Lance said. "Why try to murder me now? They don't have their money yet!"

"Well, they obviously wanted you out of the way for *some* reason," Nancy pointed out.

Suddenly Bess gave a gasp. "Or they were after you, Nan!"

"No," Nancy said. "If they'd wanted me out of the way, they would have bombed *my*—wait a minute," she whispered. "My car wouldn't start. That's why I was in the Maserati!"

She ran over to the Mustang and lifted the hood. Then her jaw tightened. She reached in and grabbed a loose wire.

"Here's the problem," she said. "Somebody pulled one of the wires off the distributor cap. Whoever did this tried to fix it so that they could get me and Lance at the same time!"

All Nancy could think was that the kidnappers must be on to her. And if they were, that made everyone's job more dangerous.

Nancy decided to keep the thought to herself. There was no point in making Bess and Lance any more scared than they already were.

"Do you have another car?" Nancy asked Lance.

He nodded. "I always keep a spare or two around," he said, winking flirtatiously at Bess.

For a minute Nancy wondered how he could joke at a time like that. But she decided he was probably just trying to lighten things up a little.

"Go on ahead to the bank," she told him. "I'll cancel the auto club and fix my car, then go to the mall. I'll get back as soon as I can."

Bess stuck to Lance like a wad of gum until he finally pulled out of the driveway. When his car was out of sight, she sighed. "I can't believe it! He was so lucky he forgot that briefcase and had to go back into the house."

"We were both lucky," Nancy reminded her.

"Ned will be so glad you're safe," Bess went on. "He must be worried sick about— Why are you looking at me like that, Nancy?"

"Ned doesn't know about this case," Nancy said, trying to sound matter-of-fact.

"He doesn't *know*? You're involved in something this big and you haven't even bothered to tell him?"

"Ned had a big paper to do this week," Nancy told her. "I just didn't want to bother him."

Now Bess sounded almost angry. "Bother him! Nancy, you know I try to stay out of your love life—"

"I know, and I'm grateful to you for doing it, Bess—"

"But don't you think he'd rather know about it when you're in danger?" Bess went on. "He won't care much about getting an A on a paper if he never gets the chance to say goodbye to you."

"Oh, stop being melodramatic, Bess!" Nancy exclaimed. "This isn't that dangerous. And I'd just like for once to give Ned a break and *not* drag him into a case."

"Not dragging him in is one thing. Not bothering to tell him someone is trying to murder you is another. I think it's kind of an insult to leave him in the dark. Wouldn't you want to know if he were in trouble?"

She would, Nancy knew.

And suddenly she realized that Ned's paper wasn't the only reason she didn't want to tell him about this case. Ned wouldn't have wanted her to take on something so dangerous without the help of the police. They would have argued about it. And Nancy just wasn't up to another confrontation with him.

74

"There's plenty of time for him to find out later," she said. Then she changed the subject. "What are you doing here anyway, Bess? Weren't you supposed to be at the mall watching George?"

"Oh! Yes. That's what I came to tell you," said Bess. "George has found that tall, skinny kid with the Mohawk. The last time I saw them, they were gazing into each other's eyes over a couple of burgers."

"So why did you leave her?"

"Well," Bess drawled, "I guess I could have called you to tell you that. But then I wouldn't have been able to see Lance."

Nancy folded her arms and stared up at the sky, fighting to keep her temper.

"You'd better be glad I didn't call," Bess said defensively. "If I hadn't shown up, we wouldn't be having this conversation now. You wouldn't be having a conversation with anyone right now—not on this earth, anyway."

"Okay, Bess," Nancy said. She glanced at her watch. With all the excitement the morning had raced by.

"I've got to get back to check on George," Nancy said. She patted Bess on the arm. "Say, would you mind staying here? Someone should be here to handle any messages that may come in—and if you see Monica, you can keep an eye on her too."

"All right," said Bess reluctantly. "But if she gives me any problems, I'm going to deck her."

"You do that," Nancy said, and laughed.

When Nancy arrived at the mall, she went into the hamburger place. George and the kid with the Mohawk were nowhere to be seen.

Nancy walked for what seemed like miles before she spotted the two. They were standing in the corridor looking into a store window. Nancy's skin crawled when the kid with the Mohawk took George's hand.

As Nancy eased her way through the crowd to get a closer look at the pair, her heart began to thunder. George could be in real danger if this boy were connected to the Hal Colson kidnapping! But Nancy held back. George knew what she was doing, and she didn't show any outward signs of nervousness.

Nancy was deciding what to do when she saw Bess coming toward her. "Bess! Why aren't you at the house?" she asked.

"This is why," answered Bess, handing Nancy a neatly folded letter.

Nancy opened it. It was on stationery with Lance's letterhead. In neat handwriting it said, "Ms. Drew: I can take care of things myself. I don't need a baby-sitter. Especially one with eyes for my man." The note was signed "Monica Sloane."

Before Nancy could say anything, Bess blurted out, "Imagine the nerve of that woman! Calling me a baby-sitter. And accusing me of—why, she almost threw me out of the house!"

Nancy was reading the note again. Absent-mindedly she ran her fingers over the fine texture of the paper.

"Well, aren't you going to say anything?" Bess asked.

Nancy barely heard the words. A half-buried memory was forcing its way to the surface, and she was struggling to identify it. The note—the notepaper . . .

After fishing through her purse, Nancy pulled out the first ransom note Lance had received. She held it up to the sun and stared at it. The paper was fine-textured linen, with a swan watermark on it.

Then Nancy held up Monica's handwritten note—and smiled wryly. "Yep," she said. Monica's note had the same watermark.

Holding the two papers side by side, Nancy saw that the ransom note was shorter than Monica's. The Colson letterhead had been cut off the ransom note.

"Nancy, what is it?" Bess asked.

Nancy grabbed Bess's arm and pointed her toward George and the guy with the Mohawk.

"You stay here and keep an eye on George," she said. "I'm going to talk to Monica Sloane!"

"Well, Monica?" asked Nancy half an hour later as she confronted Monica with Lance, who had just returned. "What's the connection between your note to Bess and Hal's ransom note? I'm sure we'd all like to know." She was watching Monica's eyes for any sign that might give her away.

"You're a stupid little thing," Monica said. She stalked across the room and threaded her arm through Lance's. "Lance, are you going to stand here and let her talk to me that way?"

Lance shook his arm free and moved toward Nancy. He was staring at Monica as if he'd never seen her before.

"I'm sorry to do this," Nancy said to him. I know it has to come as a shock to you. But Monica's a prime suspect in this kidnapping."

"And *you* are insane," snarled Monica.

"Both of you, be quiet!" Lance said, raising his voice slightly. Fighting to regain his composure, he turned to Nancy. "Nancy, I know you think this is true, but it really isn't. I know Monica. She doesn't like Hal, but she wouldn't do something like this."

Monica was smirking at Nancy from across the room. Nancy decided to ignore her. "Then how else do you explain the fact that both notes were written on your personal stationery?" she asked Lance.

"Simple. Monica got a piece of letterhead off my desk to write you that note. The other paper was probably in Hal's car. He was always borrowing my good stationery for stupid little things. We've even argued about that very thing."

The story wasn't what Nancy wanted to hear, but it made sense.

"I bet the kidnappers found some of my stationery in Hal's car," Lance continued.

Nancy nodded, but in her mind things still weren't adding up. Why would the kidnappers have bothered to cut the letterhead off the paper? What difference would it have made? If they'd deliberately intended to use this special paper, why not just use it as it was?

Nancy turned and paced the room, her back to Lance and Monica. There was no point in talking to Monica any further. And it was clear that Lance didn't share her suspicions, so she couldn't take it any further with him. But as far as she was concerned, Monica was still one of her main suspects.

Monica had all the reason in the world to want Hal out of the way. With him gone, Monica could try to put her relationship with

Lance back together again. If she could marry him, she'd be able to tap into a huge fortune—one they wouldn't have to share with Hal.

Monica began whining again and the sound broke into Nancy's thoughts. "Why don't you kick her out, Lance?" Monica asked. "She's not going to find Hal for you."

"Go upstairs, Monica," Lance answered quietly, patting her arm. "You're upset."

Monica was silent for a second. Then she started to shriek.

"Of course I'm upset!" she screamed. "You bring that little brat and her bratty little friends in here and let them walk all over me! You accuse me of kidnapping your rotten nephew! You—you—" Her face became contorted by rage. Suddenly she twisted away from Lance and grabbed a poker from the fireplace.

"I'll get you, Nancy Drew!" she screeched, charging straight at Nancy with the poker straight out in front of her.

Chapter

Nine

NANCY REACTED SWIFTLY. As Monica came toward her, she spun around and kicked the poker out of Monica's hand. It flew through the air, landing with a clatter across the room.

But that didn't stop Monica. Her eyes filled with murderous rage, she picked up a huge, ornate vase from an end table and hurled it at Nancy. Luckily, she missed—and the vase sailed onto the arm of the sofa behind Nancy. It teetered precariously for a second, then toppled safely over onto the sofa cushion. Nancy picked it up and walked over and replaced it on the end table.

"Monica! Are you crazy?" yelled Lance. "That's a Tang vase!"

"Not to mention the fact that she tried to kill me," said Nancy dryly.

Monica stared at Lance and Nancy, her jaw working. She opened her mouth, but no sound came out. Then she rushed upstairs and they heard the sound of running feet overhead, a door slamming—and then silence.

"That's the bathroom she ran into!" said Lance. "There are all kinds of pills and razors in there—and the window is right over a brick patio!"

Nancy was already halfway up the stairs.

"*That* door," said Lance as he raced up behind her. "The one down those little steps."

They stopped outside the door. There was complete silence inside.

"Monica?" Nancy called cautiously. She tried the doorknob, but it was locked.

"Monica! Are you in there?" Lance shouted. More silence.

"Can you break down the door?" Nancy whispered.

"Monica, I'm worried about you! If you don't open the door, I'm going to break the door down!" said Lance.

"I'm going to call the police," Nancy said.

"No! Don't! We don't want them in on this,

remember? She's pulled this kind of stunt before. Monica," he said, raising his voice again, "I'm going to count to three. If you don't open the door, I promise I'm going to break it down. One . . . two . . . three!"

Nothing happened.

"Okay," Lance said grimly. He rammed his shoulder against the door. And again. The door shook slightly on its hinges, but it stayed put.

"Once more," Nancy said. "It's about to give."

"So's my shoulder," grunted Lance, but he tried once more. That time the door burst open, and the two of them ran in—to an empty bathroom.

"Oh, no!" gasped Nancy. She raced to the window and looked down, dreading the sight that awaited her.

But there was no one on the patio. And no sign of anyone having jumped.

"What's going on here?" Nancy asked.

Then she saw Monica. She was standing on the ledge outside the window, just a few feet out of reach. Her eyes were wild, and she was poised to jump.

"Don't try to stop me!" she said.

Lance had rushed to Nancy's side. "Monica, come in, you idiot! Stop making a scene!" he shouted. No one's going to hurt you! Don't be ridiculous!" He turned to Nancy and said, "She's just doing it to get attention. She won't jump or anything."

"I know," Nancy whispered back to him. "But this isn't the way to get her back inside!"

"Monica," she said out loud, "I'm sorry if I upset you. I didn't mean to."

"Upset me? Upset me! You accuse me of murder and then try to apologize?"

"I wasn't accusing you of murder," Nancy said calmly. "I'm sorry if it looked that way to you. If you'll come back inside, I promise I'll stop pestering you."

Monica looked at her suspiciously.

"I promise," Nancy repeated. "Don't you know that if you're innocent, you have nothing to worry about? Now come on back inside. We don't want to hurt you." There was a long silence.

Nancy held out her hand. "See, you can just take my hand and walk back inside," she said, coaxing her.

Slowly Monica reached out and took Nancy's hand. "That's it; that's right," Nancy said, encouraging her. And she pulled Monica in through the window.

Monica sagged against the wall and slid to the floor.

"I'm so tired," she moaned. "So tired."

"Of course you are," Nancy said. "Why don't

you let Lance call someone to put you to bed? You've had a big day." She nodded over her shoulder at Lance, and he vanished down the hall.

In a second he came back with a comfortable-looking older woman. "Mrs. Bracken, my secretary," he said to Nancy. "Sorry you have to meet under these circumstances."

"Come on, Ms. Sloane," said Mrs. Bracken cheerfully. "Let's get you to bed."

As Nancy and Lance watched, Mrs. Bracken helped Monica to her feet and urged her down the hall to her bedroom. The door closed behind them.

Lance turned to Nancy. "Thank you," he said. "That's an incredible thing you just did."

"All in a day's work," Nancy said lightly. "Let's go downstairs."

"Whew!" she said when they were back in the living room. "Mind if I sit down?"

"Please do," answered Lance. "I think I will too. Well, now you know how exciting life gets around here."

"Yes," Nancy said. "You have my sympathy."

"She wouldn't really have hurt you, you know," said Lance. "She always stops herself in time. But I'm certainly glad you were here—and that you managed to keep your wits."

"Anyway, it's over now," said Nancy. "I hate

to say it, but we should get back to the main subject. Did you get the ransom money?"

Lance smiled wanly. "You know, I'd forgotten all about that. Yes, I did get it—with help from your father's office. I had to get a letter from one of his assistants in order to make the withdrawal," he said. "My banker looked at me kind of funny when I asked for four hundred and seventy-five thousand dollars in cash, but there was no problem, really."

His mention of the money reminded Nancy of something that had been nagging her since the beginning of the case. Suddenly she knew what it was.

"Why that particular amount?" she asked Lance. "Why do you think the kidnappers didn't ask for five hundred thousand dollars? Why not round it up? Four hundred and seventy-five thousand seems like such a weird figure."

"I—I never thought of that," Lance confessed. "I—maybe it just seemed like a more reasonable amount. You know—not too little, not too much. Like when something's priced at nine ninety-nine instead of ten dollars."

"It still seems odd to me," said Nancy. She sighed. "Well, I'd better get back to the mall to check on George. If Monica's not the link to this case, then George could be in a lot of danger."

"You're right," Lance said as he held the door open for her.

"Oh, and don't let Monica go anywhere. No matter what she says, and what you think, she's still a suspect in this case. I'd appreciate it if you'd find someone who can keep an eye on her for the next few days," Nancy said.

"All right."

At that minute the phone rang. Lance ran to pick it up in the foyer. "Lance Colson here," he said.

Then his eyes widened. He motioned to Nancy to get on another extension. "It's the kidnappers!" he mouthed.

Nancy raced into the den and carefully picked up the phone in there. It was George! Nancy's body turned cold as she listened.

"Noon tomorrow at the east end of the footbridge," George was saying. "Don't be late, or you'll never see Hal again."

Chapter

Ten

NANCY HUNG UP the phone and raced back into the foyer to Lance.

"That was George!" she said. "She's penetrated the kidnapping ring! Those kids I saw on the tape with Hal must be the kidnappers!"

"You mean that was your friend on the phone?" Lance asked.

"Yes." Nancy smiled. "I knew she could do it. She's great, isn't she? She convinced them to make her one of them, and now they have her making the ransom calls!"

Suddenly her enthusiasm faded. "Of course, it's also possible," she said, "that they're on to us. They may have kidnapped George too.

They may just be making her do their dirty work. But I think we'd better proceed according to what she said to you."

"Before you picked up the phone," Lance said, "she told me to go to Liberty Park. Alone. The drop is to be made at the footbridge at noon."

"I heard that last part," Nancy said. "Do exactly what she told you. If we haven't gotten Hal back by tomorrow, I'll be at the park early to see what I can do then. I'll try to follow them back to where they have Hal hidden."

Lance grabbed her arm. "But what if they get away?" he asked fiercely. "What happens then?"

Stepping back and taking a deep breath, Nancy answered, "It's my job to see that they don't get away."

Lance snorted. "That's a comfort."

Was he being sarcastic? Nancy didn't know, but his words smarted. "I guess I forgot to tell you that this wouldn't be all champagne and roses!" she snapped.

"Hey, I'm sorry. I was just kidding," Lance protested.

"Well, there's nothing to laugh about. I think you should know what I've known all along. The longer it takes to get Hal back, the greater the odds are that we'll never get him back. Alive, anyway. I know you're under a lot of pressure, but you'd better get hold of yourself. Because we're down to the wire, and if George and I can't find your nephew before tomorrow, some very serious stuff will be going down in that park tomorrow at noon."

Lance looked like a kid who'd just been yelled at by his mother. "Just tell me what you want me to do," he said quietly. "I'm on your side, remember?"

"Are you?" Nancy asked. "Sometimes it's hard to tell. Anyway, I'm leaving for the mall now. You stay here in case George or anyone else calls. I'll be in touch." And she marched out of the house.

On her way to the mall she passed Bess, who was driving in the opposite direction.

Bess started honking and waving, and Nancy pulled over to the side of the road and waited as Bess circled around to join her. Bess hopped out of her car and came running over to Nancy's.

"George left the mall with that tall, skinny guy with the Mohawk," she panted. "I tried to follow them, but a whole bunch of them were on motorcycles and in a car. They lost me in the traffic. There was nothing I could do."

"Oh, no," Nancy said, sighing.

"I think George might be in trouble!" Bess was actually wringing her hands. "What are we going to do, Nancy? I tried to follow her, just the way you said, but they were just too fast. What if they've taken her off someplace to kill her? It'll be all my fault!"

"Bess," Nancy said, getting out of her car and taking Bess by the shoulders. "Think a minute. Did George look as though she was really in trouble? Did she look as if she was being forced to leave?"

"Well, no," Bess answered. "I don't think so." She started to fidget again. "But how else can you explain it? Why would she have gone off with that bunch of creeps?"

"You know George as well as I do," Nancy said. "She sometimes tends to be a little overconfident. Maybe that's what happened." Nancy paused for a moment. "But I think that this time she may be playing a more dangerous game than she knows."

"Wait, why do you say that?" Bess asked. "I thought you weren't worried."

Nancy told Bess about the call George had made to Lance.

"George did that?" Bess gasped.

Nancy nodded. "There's no way of knowing if they're on to her or not. But one thing we do know is that they should be pretty excited about getting the money tomorrow."

"I wonder how many of them there are," said

Bess. "Four hundred and seventy-five thousand dollars could be split among a lot of people."

"I guess you're right," said Nancy. A car whizzed by, then another. "I think it would be a good idea if you'd cruise the streets tonight, Bess. See if you can spot any of those kids on bikes or in cars. And if you see George, stay with her."

Bess looked away from Nancy and lowered her head. "I think that's a good idea, Nan, but since I've already lost George once, don't you think you should handle the cruising stuff? You're better at it than I."

"You can handle it," Nancy said reassuringly. "I have to go back to the mall. I hope I can find Amy Tyler. Now that we know some of Hal's friends are involved, I think Lance may be right—Amy may be involved in the kidnapping."

The last couple hours of the afternoon passed slowly. By five o'clock Nancy had all but given up. People were starting to go home for supper, and Nancy's feet were starting to hurt.

How could I have spent so much time here and not seen something that will help? she thought. Besides spending a lot of time, she had also spent a lot of money—it was the only way to hang around in the stores without making salespeople suspicious. Nancy was now the owner of a new purse, four new pairs of socks, three records, and six magazines, unwelcome souvenirs of an unsuccessful afternoon.

Nancy had just decided it was time to quit and contact Lance again. She was heading for one of the mall exits when she saw George and the guy with the Mohawk walking hand in hand into the fast-food restaurant about ten feet from Nancy.

Her heart pounding, Nancy fell into step behind them. Once she was inside she pretended to scrutinize the overhead menu, all the while unobtrusively moving closer to George and her new "friend."

"Let's get something to drink, Sam," she heard George say. "I'm dry after being on that bike all afternoon." Sam agreed.

Nancy made her way to the closest food server. "Small cola, please," she said. George and Sam were right behind her.

"Hang on a minute," Nancy said to the waitress. "I know my wallet's here somewhere." Actually she knew exactly where it was, but she wanted to make sure George had seen her.

"Hey, hurry up, will you?" said Sam in back of her. "My girlfriend's thirsty."

"Oh, I'm sorry—wait—oh, here it is!" Nancy produced the wallet with a flourish, then turned around and flashed Sam a big smile. "Sorry," she said. "You know how it is sometimes."

"Sure I do—for morons like you," Sam answered.

George burst into exaggerated laughter. She was practically doubled over, laughing so hard she couldn't see—and then she crashed into Nancy and knocked Nancy's soda onto the floor.

"Oh!" she gasped. "Sorry." She grabbed some napkins and started wiping up the spill.

"Why bother?" asked Sam. "It wasn't your fault—it was hers for getting in the way!"

Nancy knew something was going on. But she didn't know what until, under one of the napkins, George slipped her a note.

Surprised, Nancy fumbled for a second. The note fell to the floor, and she quickly reached down to pick it up.

But before her hand could get to the note, a big dirty tennis shoe with no laces slid across the top of it.

Nancy didn't need to look up. She knew Sam had seen the whole thing. He picked up the note and put it in his shirt pocket. Quietly and without making a scene, he grabbed George by the arm and with his other hand encircled Nancy's wrist.

Through clenched teeth and a fake smile, he looked at them and said, "What's going on here?"

Chapter

Eleven

GEORGE LOOKED TOO shocked to speak. Nancy figured they'd be better off if George stayed out of it.

"That's exactly what I'd like to know. What is going on here?" Nancy said. Her voice was loud and demanding, and she saw that the sheer force of her determination made George revive a little.

Nancy glared at George. "You clumsy idiot." She was making a big thing of brushing off her skirt and wiping the sticky soda off her hands. "You punks are all alike. Think you own this mall. I would like to shop here, but animals like you are the reason *real* people are staying away from this place in droves."

"Yeah? Well, why don't you go join your drove?" Sam asked.

"Oh, forget it," said George. "This goody-goody preppy is not worth wasting our time on. Let's not let her wreck the day any more than she already has." She took Sam's arm. "She's really made a mess of everything," she said, looking down at her feet. "If she'd been watching where she was going, I wouldn't have gotten soda on my stockings."

Sam looked down at the soda splattered on George's ankles. "You going to pay to have those cleaned?" he asked Nancy.

Nancy snickered. "Have stockings cleaned? What a stupid thing to say." She wrinkled her nose at George. "Anyway, they were probably filthy to begin with."

"Let's just forget our drinks and go," George said, trying to pull Sam away with her. "She's a loser."

"You're right, babe," Sam said. "The place is full of them."

Sam grabbed George's arm and started to walk away.

He still had the note in his pocket! "Just a minute, please," said Nancy, trying not to sound too urgent. "I want my grocery list back."

"Now what are you talking about?" asked Sam.

"The list I dropped on the floor. The one you put your big dirty foot on."

Sam suddenly looked suspicious.

"I'm going to call mall security if you don't give it back right now," Nancy said. For a second she wondered what would happen if she ran into Lester Mathers again. "Come on. Cough it up."

The look in George's eyes was unmistakable. Nancy knew George would be in big trouble if anyone else read that note.

"Give her the list, babe," George whined. "And let's get out of here. She's getting on my head in a very bad way."

Sam threw George an angry glance. "I don't let my girlfriends tell me what to do!" he growled. "The sooner you learn that, the better." He took a deep breath and turned back to Nancy.

"Go ahead—call mall security. Call the police. Call the National Guard if you want. I'm not giving it back." He yanked on George's arm and looked back over his shoulder at Nancy. "Make yourself a new list, mighty mouth. You're not getting this one." He patted his pocket and grinned at her.

Nancy saw terror fill George's eyes again as the two walked away. What could she do?

She couldn't really go to mall security. Lester Mathers wouldn't buy another one of her stories, especially when she wasn't sure he'd bought the first one. And pressing Sam any further had to be a mistake.

He seemed to forget about the note until I asked for it, Nancy thought. Maybe he'll forget about it again. Maybe George can figure out a way to get it back.

Nancy dropped back and followed George and Sam through the mall. With every step she became more worried about George. What was going to happen if Sam did read the note? Nancy was sure George had been trying to tell her something about the kidnapping—and even George wouldn't be able to come up with a decent story this time.

Nancy crept along behind the pair, then suddenly stopped. George and Sam had halted just a few feet ahead of her.

They were talking to the big guy who'd been on the tape—the one who'd been talking to Sam and Hal. Seen in person, he looked like Goliath —big, mean, and dumb. Nancy inched a little closer, keeping her face away from the trio, and pretended to be window-shopping.

In a few seconds Amy Tyler had joined the group. Uh-huh, Lance was right, Nancy thought. Amy *is* in on the kidnapping.

But as she kept her eye on the group, she

began to wonder if that was really true. Amy seemed to be asking the boys something. She looked as if she was begging, in fact. And they weren't telling her what she wanted to hear.

Amy started yelling at the big guy, but Nancy couldn't understand what she was saying. She did see her wave her arms agitatedly in the air. Suddenly the big guy stepped forward and shoved her—hard. Amy reeled backward and fell to the ground. George bent to help her up, but Sam angrily yanked George back.

George looked wildly around her. Was she trying to find Nancy?

If only I were closer! Nancy thought. If only I could hear them—or at least let George know I haven't abandoned her!

But she knew she had to resist the temptation to move closer. If any one of the three kids with George saw her, it would be disastrous for George, for Nancy, and most of all for Hal.

Amy had struggled to her feet by then and was talking in a more subdued way to Sam and the other guy. Now it looked as if all four of them were going to leave together.

They were headed for the exit when Sam suddenly stopped. He stuck his hand into his pocket and pulled out the note George had tried to give Nancy.

"This is it," Nancy whispered. "I've got to help her!"

Keeping her eyes glued on Sam, she positioned herself in back of a group of girls who were moving in George's direction. She hoped they'd conceal her until she got close enough.

Sam took Goliath to one side and opened the note. By this time Nancy was close enough to see all she needed. Sam's and Goliath's faces turned white, then red. Nancy couldn't tell whether their expressions were ones of horror, fear, or just plain rage.

Amy strode up to the two guys. She looked as if she were demanding to know what was going on. That was when Goliath shoved her down again, but this time George ran over to Amy and picked her up.

Nancy didn't want to see Amy get hurt, but the move was just what she needed to get closer. A crowd was beginning to gather around Amy and George. But just before Nancy could join it, Sam grabbed George's arm, Goliath grabbed Amy's, and the two guys dragged the girls outside.

Nancy raced to the exit. They couldn't get away! She couldn't let them hurt George! She and her friends had been in some tough situations before, but this time she'd gotten George in over her head. If only I'd figured out a way to handle it myself! she thought.

Nancy dashed out the exit and into the dusky light. George was standing right in front of her—and George looked as if she were about to faint.

Nancy didn't have time to ask, "Are you all right?" A sharp blow landed on the back of her head. And she heard George scream as her world went black.

Chapter
Twelve

SOMEWHERE THERE WAS a light that was much too bright. Nancy groaned and slowly opened her eyes, narrowing them immediately into slits. The light came from a bare bulb in a dirty ceiling overhead, and Nancy was lying on the floor just under it.

She sat up, rubbed her throbbing temples, and surveyed her surroundings. George was lying on the floor next to her, and Amy Tyler was in a chair across from them. It looked as though they were in a small apartment—the filthiest, most depressing apartment Nancy had ever seen.

"Are you all right?" whispered George.

Nancy nodded.

Sam must have heard them. He crossed the room in three steps and stood above them menacingly.

He was holding a gun.

"All right," he said. "I want to know what kind of game you three are playing. If you know what's good for you, you'll talk." Slowly he swiveled the gun so it pointed at each of them in turn.

But before any of the girls could speak, he added, "It's all over. You know that, don't you? Whatever your game is, it's all over now."

George straightened up and threw him a longing look. "I'm not playing a game, Sam!" she said tearfully. She turned to stare at Nancy and Amy. "I don't know who these two are. I've never seen them before today!"

"No?" Sam said. "Then what about that note? You remember that little thing—the note telling where Hal was? How'd that happen to drop on the floor at your feet?"

"I wish I knew. Believe me, I wish I knew," said George.

"Someone gave it to me," Nancy said firmly.

But they hadn't been planning on Amy's reaction. She jumped out of her chair, slapping Sam's gun out of her way, and bent over George.

"You're a fool," she told Sam. "And I'm one too." She grabbed George's face and pushed her hair back. "I knew she looked familiar!" she said. "And this girl is a friend of hers."

Sam trained the gun on Nancy. Without moving, he asked, "Who is she?"

"A friend of Monica Sloane's, Lance Colson's girlfriend."

Sam's gun hand was trembling. Nancy didn't know if it was from nerves or anger. Whatever the reason, she did know that his trembling hand was far more dangerous than a steady one.

He was staring down at George now. "I thought you liked me," he said. "I thought we could be something special together."

"We still can be," pleaded George.

"Shut up!" Sam shouted, turning the gun in her direction. "You didn't like me. You never liked me. You just wanted to find out about Hal Colson!"

Nancy's pulse quickened. They had to find a way out of there before Sam hurt somebody. His hand was trembling more with each passing second, and sweat was pouring off his face.

"Come here, Jed," he said to the guy Nancy called Goliath. "Hold the gun on these two until I decide what to do with them. Feel free to use it if they cause any trouble."

Sam passed the gun to Jed. Jed wasn't trembling. His grip was steady, sure, and straight—and the little grin at the corner of his mouth told Nancy all she wanted to know about Jed and guns. He had shot before—and liked it. He'd probably be delighted to have an excuse to shoot someone again.

"Please, please tell me where Hal is," Amy begged Sam. She grabbed his hand and stared searchingly into his face. "Where's he hiding? What have you guys done with him?"

"Will you just *shut up?*" snapped Sam. "I'm trying to think!"

Amy's eyes filled with tears. "I thought we were all friends. I thought you liked Hal. You've hurt him, haven't you? I know you have! What are you going to do now? Get rid of me the way you've gotten rid of him?"

"Well, that eliminates one suspect, Nan," George said quietly to Nancy.

"True," answered Nancy. "She obviously doesn't know where Hal is."

Amy gave them a look of pure hatred, then she burst into tears.

"SHUT UP!" bellowed Sam. "Will the three of you keep quiet for a second?"

Nancy's head was still throbbing, but she knew she had to ignore it. Sam was practically twitching with nerves, and Jed looked as though he were just waiting for the signal to blow them away. The situation was about as dangerous as it was ever going to get, and Nancy needed a plan. Right then.

Suddenly there were footsteps at the back door. A key turned in the lock. The door opened—and in walked Hal Colson!

"Hal!" Amy shrieked, running to him and throwing her arms around his neck. "I've been so worried. I thought you were dead!"

"Do I look it?" asked Hal with a grin. He certainly didn't. He looked fit, healthy, and relaxed—completely different from the terror-stricken boy in the ransom photo.

Amy was so excited she was laughing and crying at the same time. "Lance told me you'd gone to visit your grandmother in Michigan, but I just knew that had to be a lie," she said, babbling on. "I was out of my mind! I just couldn't stop thinking about you! I decided I wouldn't give up until I'd found you. I'm so glad you're all right!" She grabbed his head and kissed him.

Hal took her hands and gently pulled them away. Then he smiled at her and kissed her on the forehead. "I didn't want to get you involved, Amy," he said. "I would have told you, but I wanted to surprise you with the money."

He slipped his arms around her and gave her a hug. "I was just going to show up at your door later today with a bagful of money and two tickets to the West Coast."

Amy's mouth dropped open. Her eyes were round with amazement.

"I know how much you like the ocean," Hal said tenderly. "I thought we could spend some time in California, just surfing and hanging out on the beach."

"That would be wonderful," said Amy, squeezing him around the waist. "But don't ever surprise me like this again." She put her head on his chest, then looked up into his eyes. "I was insane. I even went to Lester Mathers to see if he'd seen you."

Hal started to laugh. "That old guy? What did *he* tell you?"

"Don't laugh," Amy said, pouting. "He told me not to worry. He said people like you always landed on their feet."

"I don't know if he meant it as a compliment, but he was right." Hal grinned cockily at her.

"Know what else Lester told me?" asked Amy.

Hal just smiled and shook his head.

"He said his mother had died and left him a lot of money. He's going to quit his job in two weeks and just travel and do what he wants."

So that was it. That was the conversation Nancy had heard outside Lester's office. It had been *Amy* talking. Her words played through Nancy's memory again. "Soon this will all be over, and you'll be a rich man." Of course. "This" meant working for a living.

"We're going to do just what he's going to do," Hal said. "Travel and do what we want. Only we aren't going to have to wait until we're fifty to do it. We won't even have to wait for two weeks."

Amy tipped her head to one side and gave him a puzzled look. "But, Hal, where are we going to get the money?"

"Yes, Hal," Nancy broke in. "What's your next move?"

For the first time Hal seemed to notice her. "What's it to you?" he asked, scowling. "I don't know who you are, babe, but if you've messed up getting my money, I'll have my friend here make you wish you hadn't." He nodded at Jed, who winked coyly at Nancy and pushed the gun even closer to her head.

Now the pieces of the puzzle were finally coming together. *"Your* money?" Nancy asked thoughtfully. "The ransom money's coming to you? So that's it. This kidnapping was all a ploy!"

"That's right, smart girl," Hal answered. He stepped closer to her. "And now that you know so much about me, how about saying a little something about yourself? You can start by telling me who you are."

"My name is Nancy Drew," Nancy said coldly. "I'm a private detective. I was asked by your uncle Lance to investigate your kidnapping."

"Good old Lance! Always thinking of me." Hal chuckled.

"I was asked to find you and foil the ransom attempt," Nancy continued.

"I should have known! Lance would do anything to keep from paying my money." He smirked at Nancy. "Too bad it's not going to work the way you two had things planned. I hate him and he hates me," Hal said. "I don't know why he didn't just leave things alone. It was a perfect setup—he would have been rid of me forever. Or at least for a while."

Nancy couldn't understand Hal's attitude. "Your uncle is worried sick about you," she said. "What's your problem, anyway?" She knew it was an unprofessional question, but Hal was really irritating her.

"My problem?" Hal threw his hands into the air and let them fall at his sides. "My *problem* is my uncle," he said. "Lance is the stingiest guardian alive. I have to wait until I'm twenty-five before I can even touch my own money. Who wants to wait that long? I've got things to do between now and then, and it's going to take a little cash."

Hal patted Jed on the back. "So I made a deal with three of my friends. I'd pretend to be kidnapped. We'd collect, share the money, and then Amy and I would be off for the sunny California coast."

Nancy closed her eyes for a second. She couldn't believe what she was hearing. Poor Lance! she thought. How did he put up with a kid like this?

Sam was still in the chair he'd collapsed into after turning the gun over to Jed. Suddenly he stood up and started walking in agitated circles. He was still shaking, and he looked pale.

"Something bad is going to happen," he said to Hal. "We're all going to get caught. I know it." He grabbed Hal's shirt. "We're going to get caught, and then we're going to jail."

"We're not—"

"I don't want to go to jail, man!" Sam interrupted, kicking a chair violently. "I wish I'd never let you talk us into this!"

Jed darted a glance over his shoulder at Sam. Quickly he turned back to Nancy and George— but Nancy could tell he was listening hard.

"We were just goofing around, having some fun," Sam said. "Now look at all the trouble we're in."

"That's right!" George said. "You're not going to like prison," she added sweetly.

"No more talking, doll," Jed ordered.

"Oh, please excuse me," answered George.

Hal took Sam by the shoulders and forced

him to stop pacing. "For the last time," he said slowly and distinctly, "we are not going to get caught. We have the detective and her partner here. They aren't going to mess up our plans. And Lance is probably too scared to do anything but what we've told him to do. Everything's going to happen just the way we planned."

Sam was calmer now. Hal walked with him to the sofa.

"Once we get our hands on that seventy-five grand, and I give you your share, you're going to be real glad you were in on this deal," Hal said.

Seventy-five thousand? Nancy and George stared at each other.

"What did you plan to do with the other four hundred thousand, Hal?" asked Nancy.

Hal turned to look at her. Sam, Jed, and Amy turned to look at him.

His face had lost a little of its color and a lot of its glow.

"What four hundred thousand?" he asked.

Chapter

Thirteen

You ASKED FOR four hundred and seventy-five thousand dollars in your first ransom note," Nancy said. "Don't tell me you don't remember it, Hal. The one that was done up all nice and neat on your uncle's stationery?"

"The one with those cute little photos of you in it," George added.

Nancy picked up her purse and started to open it. "Here," she said. "I'll show you."

Jed's gun was between Nancy's eyes before she could get the clasp open.

"Call off your friend," Nancy ordered. "I'm not going to do anything stupid. I just thought you might have forgotten what that four-hundred-and-seventy-five-thousand-dollar note looked like. I've got it here in my purse to remind you."

Hal looked at both girls suspiciously. "Step back and let her get the note," he ordered Jed.

But when Nancy pulled the ransom note from her purse, Sam snapped. Leaping to his feet, he lunged at Nancy and grabbed the note from her hand.

"Hey, give me that!" Hal ordered, reaching for it.

Sam snatched it out of his way. "You just stay where you are, rich boy!" he said. He showed the note to Jed. Then he read it out loud—slowly, as if he couldn't believe his eyes.

"Four hundred and seventy-five thousand. She's right," he said. He looked at Jed. "I think it's time to hold the gun on our friend Hal," he said. "Our *cheating* friend Hal."

Jed finally spoke. "You should have known better than to try and cheat us, man. You had this planned all along, didn't you? Giving us a measly third of seventy-five thousand *to split three ways*. One third to me, one third to Sam, one third to Dracula for taking the pictures. Then you take your fifty thousand plus four hundred more."

"A real friend," George said. She looked at Sam. "I think you've both been had."

Sam shook his head. "No, this deal's not over yet." He glared at Hal. "With a payoff of almost half a million, a third of twenty-five thousand isn't worth getting caught for. I say we up the stakes. How about you?" he asked Jed.

Hal moved toward his two friends. "You guys have got to believe me. I don't know where that note came from. I'm not trying to put anything over on anybody but my uncle. I swear!"

"Notice he didn't offer to give you any more of his money," Nancy said, egging them on.

Jed raised the gun slightly. "Just stay where you are, Hal."

Nancy was waiting for the time to make a move. She knew Jed would soon get himself into a position where she could grab the gun without hurting anyone in the process.

She was also keeping an eye on Amy, who had curled up on the sofa. It looked as though she was trying very hard to keep out of everything that was going on. Maybe Amy really hadn't known about any of this. Sometimes she looked as shocked as Nancy felt about the things the three guys in the room were saying.

Just stay out of my way, Amy, Nancy thought. When the time comes we may all get out of here alive.

Hal turned to Sam. "You were with me when I snuck into the house and put that first ransom note on Lance's desk," he said. "Don't you remember? It was written on notebook paper. Not that fancy stuff." He pointed to the note in Sam's hand. "It was like the one we left in the car that day."

"I remember," Jed put in unexpectedly. "We all sat here at the table cutting words out of magazines so we could do both ransom notes at the same time."

"Exactly," Hal said.

Sam looked at Hal suspiciously. "I remember sneaking back into the mansion to leave that first note. But that doesn't mean you didn't have two notes with you when we went in. Maybe you just switched them when I wasn't looking."

"And how would I have done that?" Hal asked. "We had the photos with the notebook-paper note. You both know we didn't have two sets of pictures. Dracula took only one set. You guys were here when he did it!" Hal shook his head. "I couldn't take my own picture. Give me a break."

He tugged at his hair in frustration. "First there was the ransom note we left on Lance's desk," he said to himself. "On notebook paper," he emphasized to Sam. "Then there was that second note we left on the skeleton in my car." He was starting to sound more confident. "Remember, Dracula stole that blood from the blood bank and we threw it all over the car?"

Sam nodded. "Then she"—he pointed at George—"called Lance and told him to meet us at the footbridge."

Hal frowned at George. "She didn't give us away, did she?"

Jed and Sam both shook their heads.

Hal started to pace. Then he said, "I know that if we stay calm, everything is going to be all right."

"I hope so," Nancy whispered to George. She was pretty sure that her definition of "all right" wasn't the same as Hal's.

Suddenly Amy jumped off the couch. "Everything is not going to be all right," she said breathlessly. "I just thought of something."

She gestured to Nancy and George sitting on the floor. "Those two have a friend," she said. "Someone who's working with them."

"*What?*" Hal asked.

"It's true," Amy said. "I've seen all three of them snooping around the mall together." She pointed at George. "That's how I knew who *she* was. The first time I saw her, Nancy Drew was sneaking up on Dracula. I stopped her, but before I could say anything her two sidekicks were behind her."

Amy looked desperate. "I'm telling you, Hal,

there's another one who's probably looking for these two right now. And I bet she's going to try to mess up the money drop."

"That's it," Sam said confidently. "I'm not waiting for your uncle to call in the cops." He strode to the front door and opened it.

"Stop!" Hal ordered.

Sam wasn't listening. "Dracula!" he called down the stairs. "Get in here."

Dracula came springing into the apartment. Nancy wasn't surprised to see that he was the same kid she'd tried to follow at the mall.

"Hey, dudes, what's happening?" he asked jauntily.

"Hal tricked us, that's what," answered Sam.

"That's not true!" cried Hal.

"Just shut up, rich boy," snapped Jed.

"We're not waiting until noon for the money," Sam explained to Dracula.

"Far out!" said Dracula, clapping his hands. "What's the plan?"

"I want you to go to a pay phone and call Lance Colson," Sam told him.

"But we can call him from here."

"No. I don't want anybody to be able to trace any of our calls back here," Sam said. "Tell Colson to have the money at the footbridge in exactly one hour."

Nancy glanced at her watch. Seven-thirty A.M. *I must have been unconscious for several* hours, she thought for a second. Then she realized that they might just get away with it because of the time change.

"Tell him to be there in an hour or he'll never see his nephew or the detective he hired again," Sam added.

Dracula stared at him. "You mean we really might have to kill somebody? I didn't think that was part of the plan." His voice was quivering. "I thought we were just going to make it look as though we had."

"We've got a new plan now," said Sam. "I'm in charge. You just do what I tell you. And then meet us back here—wait outside."

Dracula still looked scared. But he managed an "okay" and left the apartment.

Sam closed the door behind him and turned back to Hal—a cold, clear, calculating look in his eye.

"I guess you heard that," he said. "I'm in charge now."

Hal clenched his teeth. "Like hell you are."

Hal lunged for Sam. But before Nancy could see what had happened, a gunshot blast filled the apartment, and time stood still.

Chapter
Fourteen

NANCY SPRANG TO her feet.

"Hold it!" Jed hollered. "Or you'll get the next one!"

Hal Colson was slumped over in a chair holding his arm. Blood was seeping through his fingers. From where she was standing, Nancy couldn't get a good look at the wound. But she knew that even a surface wound could be serious if enough blood was lost.

"Hal! Oh, my God!" Amy shrieked. "Are you crazy?" she shouted at Jed. "You could have killed him!"

"I could still kill you," Jed said offhandedly. But Sam reached over and plucked the gun from Jed's hand. "Who elected you president of this club?" he said disgustedly. *"I'll* take care of this. You just tie them all up. The ropes are in the kitchen."

Nancy didn't want to let that happen. She thought for a second about making a move on Sam, but there was no telling what he or any of them might do next. Nancy couldn't risk getting someone killed. She'd just have to wait for a better opportunity.

"You'll never get away with this, you know," she said.

"She's right," George told Sam. "Why don't you be sensible while there's still time?"

Sam swung the gun in her direction. "Is this your heart talking, babe? Or is it just your detective head?"

"Don't be a fool," said Nancy. "Just take a second and think about this. You haven't really done anything—yet. But once you take that money, the cops will get you for blackmail and kidnapping. And you can't even be sure you'll get the money. How do you know Lance won't figure out a way to trap you?"

Hal winced. Jed had jerked his wounded arm behind him and begun tying him to a chair.

"Stop that!" Amy cried, struggling in the chair where she was already tied. "Can't you see he needs a doctor?"

Blood from Hal's arm was dripping onto the

floor beside him. His face was growing whiter by the second. Nancy wondered how long he'd be able to remain conscious.

"Look!" she said, pointing at Hal. "You almost have a murder on your hands!"

But Jed acted as though he hadn't heard a word she said. He grabbed her hands and pulled them behind her back, then forced her into another chair. In a few seconds he had finished tying her up and started working on George.

"You're smart guys," George said helplessly. "Don't do this."

Sam looked at her with mock sympathy. "You're breaking my heart." He bent down and kissed her on the cheek. "It's too bad it had to come to this—especially after all we've meant to each other." And he and Jed started to laugh.

Hal jerked his arms, trying to break free, then fell back in his chair exhausted by the effort. "I should have known better than to trust you guys."

"Yeah, I was thinking the same thing," Sam answered. "You never were one of us, really. Just a rich kid who wanted to play."

Hal's head was drooping lower and lower. "Nothing is turning out the way I planned," he said weakly. "All I wanted was fifty thousand dollars of my *own* money to go to the West Coast."

"With me," Amy added.

Hal nodded.

Nancy still couldn't figure out the money aspect of the case. Why should someone who was heir to a fortune only want fifty thousand dollars?

"Why only fifty?" she asked. Visions of the Colson mansion, Lance's Maserati, Hal's Mercedes, and the trip to Saint-Tropez floated through her head. "Lance probably would have spent a couple of thousand dollars on you on that trip to Saint-Tropez."

"What trip?" Amy asked.

Oops! Nancy thought. Had she said something she shouldn't have? Maybe Amy—like Monica—hadn't been part of the Colsons' travel plans.

Then Hal repeated, "Yeah, what trip to Saint-Tropez? This is the first I've heard of it."

"What trip?" Nancy looked at him in disbelief. "Lance showed me a travel brochure to Saint-Tropez," she said. "He told me you two were planning a vacation there to patch things up between you."

Hal rolled his eyes. "I can't believe it! I never realized he was such a creative guy."

"What do you mean?" Nancy asked.

Hal looked at her and George. "I've been watching you two. Up until now I thought you were pretty smart."

"Up until now?"

Suddenly Hal seemed to have revived. "A vacation to Saint-Tropez. That'll be the day. My uncle would never spend that kind of money on me. He'd never take me on a vacation with him. Never in a million years," he gabbled feverishly.

He turned to Amy. "Remember that time I asked him if I could go on the school ski weekend?" he asked her. "He said no, not until I knew the meaning of a dollar. Since—since the day my parents died, he's never let me go anywhere on vacation—much less let me go on one of *his* vacations."

There was a new kind of pain in his eyes then. Nancy was beginning to think he was telling the truth.

But if Lance hadn't really been planning the trip, why had he bothered to tell her he was? Was there more to this than met the eye?

It was time to look at the pieces of the case again. Nancy was sure she had considered all the angles—but maybe she had overlooked something.

She thought about the first ransom note she had seen, the one on Lance's stationery. Monica had sworn she had had no part in it. So had Hal. Then whose note was it?

Monica's? She hated Hal. She had told Nancy all about the financial trouble at Colson Enterprises. Hal's? He hated Lance. He only wanted fifty thousand dollars out of this.

The pieces didn't add up. If Hal hadn't known about the Saint-Tropez trip, and Monica hadn't known about the Saint-Tropez trip, why had Lance been considering the trip at all? Especially when the company was having money trouble?

Lance had to be involved in this case. But how could he have been? His car had been bombed! *Someone* had wanted *him* out of the way!

Then Nancy caught her breath. Lance hadn't been anywhere near the car when the bomb had gone off. He'd been in the house getting his briefcase—*after* he'd turned his key in the ignition. Was that just a coincidence? Now that she really thought about it, Nancy realized she'd never investigated anything related to Lance Colson. She had trusted him from the beginning.

But now at last it was clear who was behind all this. It was hard to believe, but Lance must have been calling the shots all the time—right from the beginning. Why, he must have even run her car off the road!

Nancy had to get to him. Confront him. Let him know that he'd been caught.

She tried to stand up, but the ropes pulled her back into the chair.

"Untie me!" she ordered.

Jed just looked at her.

George stared at her as though she'd gone insane.

Nancy scooted her chair across the floor and right up to Sam. "Untie me," she insisted. "Or I'll—"

"Or you'll what?" asked Sam, his finger on the trigger of the gun.

"Or I'll see that when you're all caught, you'll spend the rest of your lives in jail."

"Wow, what a scary thought," Sam said sarcastically.

Jed smiled and shook his head. "I think we might as well go and get that four hundred and seventy-five grand, and then we can worry about jail."

Sam stared at Nancy first, then at George, then at Hal, and last at Amy. A new calmness seemed to have settled over him.

"I think you're right," he said slowly. He turned to Nancy. "We're going to go collect the money. Then we're going to come back and kill all of you."

Chapter

Fifteen

N o!" GEORGE SHOUTED.

"Don't tell me what to do!" Sam shouted back. "You're going to be the first one to go. You had too good a time making fun of me— pretending to like me. And no one gets away with that! If you two had just stayed out of this," he continued, "everything would have been all right."

"Yeah," Jed chimed in. "Why'd you have to go and ruin things? We never planned to hurt anybody. Without you guys, we never would have *had* to hurt anybody."

"Do you really think you have the guts to kill us all?" Hal asked weakly.

"That's the *only way* they'd ever get away with this," Amy said.

Great! Nancy thought. Thanks for pointing that out, Amy!

"Don't worry, Amy," said Hal. "They'll never do it."

Sam was starting to get nervous again. Once more the gun in his hand was trembling. "Let's get out of here," he said. "We've got some money to pick up."

"What are we going to do with *them?*" Jed asked.

Quickly Sam checked the knots on the ropes. "They'll be all right until we get back." And he and Jed walked out the door.

The four captives listened as Sam and Jed walked down the stairs. Out on the street, a car door slammed. Another one. And then a third —Dracula. The car started up and drove away.

When the sound of the engine couldn't be heard anymore, Nancy started struggling to free herself.

"Sorry about all this," she muttered to George.

"*You're* sorry! I was afraid I was going to get you killed last night at the mall."

"Part of the deal," Nancy said.

She glanced over at Hal. He was slumped over in his chair. His breathing was shallow, his complexion pasty. "I'm going to kill Lance," Hal sat up suddenly and mumbled.

He's just figured it out, Nancy thought. Too bad it took us so long.

Hal made another futile attempt to jerk free of the ropes. He fell back into his bloody chair and whispered, "Sam and Jed are fools."

"Let them take the money," Amy said soothingly.

"There won't be any," Hal said. "Lance will probably be long gone. Maybe he's even out of the country by now."

"That's probably what he was going to do with the extra four hundred thousand he added to the ransom note," Nancy said.

"I bet he's headed for Saint-Tropez right now," George added.

"And he'll get there, too, if we don't stop him!" Nancy said, pulling against the ropes again.

"Hey!" George shouted as she gave a quick lunge and stood up. The ropes fell limp around her.

"All right!" Nancy cheered. "Hurry up and untie me. We've got a plane to stop!"

Once Nancy was free, she and George untied Hal and Amy. "Let's get out of here," Nancy said, leading the way to the door.

George and Amy supported Hal and helped him across the floor.

Once outside Nancy saw that they'd been held prisoner in a garage apartment, which was near a large two-story house. She glanced around the yard for a second and saw someone dart behind a tree.

"Come on out," she shouted bravely.

"Nancy?" the voice from behind the tree called. "Is that you?"

"Bess!" George shrieked.

But who was that stepping out from behind Bess?

"Ned!" Nancy gasped and ran into his arms. "But how—when—"

Bess was looking a little shamefaced. "You told me to use my judgment," she said nervously. "Well, I did. My judgment told me to call Ned before I did anything else. So I called him at three o'clock yesterday afternoon. He drove here to help. I didn't know if either of us would ever see you again. I-I'm sorry, Nancy."

Nancy leaned back against Ned and sighed. "Well, let's talk about it later," she said. "I'm awfully glad to see you—*both* of you. How did you find us anyway?"

"I got worried about you," Bess said. "I went to the mall to look for you. It was after twelve by this time, and I just walked around to all the different doors to see if I could find either of your cars in the parking lot. I saw yours there, Nancy, and then I really got scared."

Bess pulled something from her purse. "I kept looking around for hours for signs of a fight—anything that might be a clue. I was desperate, but I finally found this by the door." She handed a folded paper to Nancy.

It was the note George had tried to give Nancy at the mall—the note describing where the apartment was!

George shook her head in wonder. "Those guys must have dropped it during the scuffle with me and Amy. Just before you got clobbered, Nancy—remember?"

Nancy rubbed the back of her head. "How could I forget?"

"I went to Ned's house to meet him at six o'clock. I didn't want to come without him," Bess said. "I parked down the road and we sneaked over."

"We were just about to storm the place when we saw those two guys come walking out," Ned said. "So *that's* the kind of people you hang out with when I'm not around!" he added teasingly.

"To tell the truth, I'm glad those two left," Bess confessed. "Ned or no Ned, I'm not big on heroic rescue attempts."

Nancy patted Bess on the arm. "Well, you

sure acted pretty heroically." She looked around the yard. Bess's car was parked in the street, and a motorcycle was parked next to the garage. It wasn't much, but it would have to do.

"Now let's get moving," Nancy said. "Hal's losing a lot of blood, and we have to stop Lance."

"Lance!" Bess exclaimed. "Stop Lance from what?"

"From stealing Hal's money," Nancy said. "And running off to Saint-Tropez."

"I don't believe it!" answered Bess. "He'd never do anything to hurt Hal."

"It's true," said Nancy. "I'm sorry, Bess, you'll just have to trust me on this one."

She turned to George and Amy. Hal seemed to be slipping in and out of consciousness. "Bess, you take Hal and Amy to the hospital in your car," Nancy ordered.

"No! If you think Lance is involved in this, I want to go with you," Bess said stubbornly.

"Bess—get the car! This kid needs help *now.*"

Nancy couldn't remember when she had seen such anger in Bess's eyes. It hurt her to know that Bess didn't believe her. "I know it's hard to accept," she said more gently. "But the important thing now is to get Hal to the hospital. You don't want to be around Lance. Trust me. Ned, would you give Amy and George a hand with Hal?"

Ned stepped forward and carefully picked Hal up in his arms. "Come on," he said. "Let's get you out of here."

As they headed for the car, Nancy ran back into the garage apartment. It was time to let the police know what was going on.

Fortunately, the policeman who answered the phone was Sergeant Tom Robinson. Nancy had dealt with him a couple of times on previous cases, and he was a friend of her father's. She knew she wouldn't have to waste time getting him to take her seriously.

"Two guys, that's right," she said into the receiver. "No, probably three guys. One has a Mohawk haircut, another is huge—a Goliath type—you can't miss any of them. Pick them up at the east end of the footbridge in Liberty Park. Thanks, Tom. I promise I'll explain this all later."

She hung up the phone and rushed back outside in time to see Ned, George, and Amy loading Hal into Bess's car.

"Take Hal and Amy to the hospital," Nancy told Ned and Bess.

"But where are you and George going?" asked Bess.

George had jumped on the motorcycle and

was firing it up. Nancy ran over to the bike and leaped on behind George.

"Nancy!" Ned yelled.

"We're going to the airport. There's no point in your coming with us, Ned," Nancy shouted over the noise of the engine. "You wouldn't recognize Lance. Come on, George, let's get going. I hope we're not too late."

Chapter

Sixteen

It was almost nine o'clock as Nancy and George arrived at the small River Heights airport. Nancy brought the motorcycle to a screeching halt outside the main entrance. "Come on! We have to hurry!" she said as she and George jumped off.

They dashed inside the airport and then stopped, frantically glancing up and down the corridor. Lance didn't appear to be among the few people milling around.

"He's got to be here!" Nancy exclaimed. "I know I've got to be right on this one."

"I know it too," George said. "We'll find him."

Nancy looked to her left. There were ticket counters spread out for about three airline carriers, and it looked as though there were a couple of more to her right.

"Let's split up," Nancy said. "I'll go this way"—she nodded to the left—"and you go that way."

"What do I do if I find him?" George asked.

"Just make some kind of commotion," Nancy said. "I'll do the same. That'll be the signal to come running."

Nancy hurried down the airport corridor, stopping at each ticket counter to check it out. All of the reservation clerks were maddeningly calm and unhurried, and none of them remembered Lance. Had she been wrong about all this?

She turned and headed back to where she and George had split up. George was walking back in her direction.

"I checked with everyone, but no one has seen him," George said as Nancy approached. "How about you?"

"No luck either," Nancy said. "Let me check the flight board for a second."

She scanned it anxiously. One of the airlines that wasn't open yet did have a direct flight to New York though. "He could take that and then get a flight to France. Let's hang around for a while. Maybe he'll show up. It's the only flight, since there's no way he can fly from here to France. This isn't an international airport."

"What time does the flight leave?" George asked.

"In about an hour."

"He could be planning to get on it at the last minute," George said.

Nancy hated to admit it even to herself, but she was getting discouraged. "George," she began—and just then the terminal's automatic doors opened. Lance was walking in. With Bess!

"Oh, no," Nancy whispered, touching George's hand and nodding in Lance's direction.

"What's she doing here?" George muttered.

The girls stood up. "Do we tackle him, or what?" George said.

But Lance had already spotted them. He ushered Bess over to them and genially indicated to Bess that she should sit down. "Don't try anything," he said calmly to Nancy and George, "or it'll be the end of your friend here."

"Bess!" George said between clenched teeth. "I thought Nancy told you to go to the hospital with Hal and Amy and Ned. What happened?"

Bess looked down at the floor. "I dropped them off with Ned. Then I went over to Lance's to get his side of the story. When I asked him about it, he"—she gave Nancy a pleading look —"he just said, 'Good timing,' and pulled me into the car with him. He was all packed and ready to go to Saint-Tropez—just as you'd guessed, Nan."

Nancy knew it was no use remonstrating with Bess then. They were all in it together, and she had to find a way out.

"I can't believe you're doing this," she said to Lance. "What makes you think you're going to get away with it?"

Lance smiled. "I'll get away with it. It's going to be even easier now than I'd planned. I've got Bess here to help me."

Bess looked up at him. "Don't do this, Lance," she begged. "It's not worth it. You'll be ruining your whole life."

Lance shook his head. "No, you're wrong. I *spent* my whole life working and doing the right thing, but I never had *real* money. That always belonged to Michael, my Midas brother. Everything he touched turned to gold."

Lance chuckled to himself. "When Michael died, and I inherited control of Colson Enterprises, I realized how great it was to have money. *Lots* of money," he added. "But unfortunately that money wasn't really mine. It was the corporation's."

"But you had a successful business of your

138

own before you took over at Colson Enterprises," Nancy said. "You told me so."

"It was nothing compared to the money Michael had." Lance moved up closer to Bess and smiled. "When I found that ransom note on the desk, it was the best day of my life. I realized that I could change it—and borrow a little of Hal's inheritance."

"You're a slime," George said.

"A *rich* slime," answered Lance. "I have almost half a million dollars with me now, courtesy of Hal's trust fund. It's mine to use as I please." He glanced over his shoulder at the ticket counter. "And in a few minutes, I'll board that plane for New York and then on to Saint-Tropez."

Nancy looked around and wondered if there was any way to tip off the airport security as to what was going on. But at the moment she didn't see anyone. Maybe if she could stall Lance long enough, she would figure out what to do.

"I guess you had everything figured out from the start," she said humbly. "I'm just sorry it took me so long to get wise to you. You must have thought I was pretty slow."

"Don't feel bad," Lance said. "You're good. You're very good. You just got outfoxed." He stared into Nancy's eyes. "I knew you would be trouble the minute your father mentioned your name. You have quite a reputation. I tried to scare you off the case by running you off the road that first night you came to see me.

"When it didn't even faze you," Lance went on, "I knew you'd be harder to handle than I'd expected. And when Monica accidentally knocked you down the stairs and even *that* didn't slow you down, I knew I'd met a worthy opponent."

"You're staying with the story that that was an accident?" Nancy asked.

"It was. Monica has never been in on this— she's too stupid. Although I'll admit, that stair business was perfect. And then the stunt with the poker! I couldn't have planned it better myself. She really came through for me, poor little fool.

"My best idea, though," said Lance, "was the bomb in the car." He sighed. "That was the supreme sacrifice. I loved that car."

"Greedy people will do anything," George said.

Ignoring her, Lance continued. "See, I knew a bomb in the car would look as though someone was after me. And it would also get you out of the way—permanently."

Nancy had heard enough. She stepped closer to Lance.

"Let Bess go," she said. "This is your last chance to give yourself up."

"No, Nancy Drew," Lance said. "In a while I'm going to get on that plane and fly off." He beamed at her and George. "There's no way anyone can stop me."

"We'll have you stopped in New York," said George.

"I don't think so. You don't know what I have planned for you before I leave."

Now! Nancy thought to herself. She reached down for Bess's hand to pull her out of her chair and away from Lance.

But Lance jerked Bess back into the seat and pulled the pistol from his coat pocket. "Get back!" he ordered, as he went over to stand beside her.

He jabbed the gun into her ribs. "None of you make a sound!" he ordered. "Another trick like that, and your friend is dead."

Chapter
Seventeen

TIME HAD RUN out. If Nancy was ever going to make a move, it had to be right then.

"Don't worry, Bess," she said soothingly. She stepped forward and reached a hand out to comfort her friend.

Then she looped her foot behind Lance's leg and pulled him off balance.

Seizing the moment, Bess broke free.

George rushed in and gave Lance a karate kick in the hand, which sent his pistol flying up into the air.

Nancy raced after the gun. She swooped it up before Lance managed to regain his balance.

Quickly George slammed Lance again with another karate kick. This time she knocked him totally prone onto the floor.

Nancy positioned herself over Lance as he lay motionless. Holding the gun on him, she said, "Now. *You* don't move."

Lance grinned up at her. "I wonder why I think you won't really pull that trigger?"

"Don't even bother wondering about it," George advised.

"Yeah," Bess chimed in. "She'd pull it in a minute if she had to."

Nancy smiled back at Lance. "Trust us. We never stop until a case is wrapped up."

"And it won't be long now," Bess said. She pointed down the corridor. "Here comes the cavalry."

Nancy took her eyes off Lance only long enough to see four River Heights policemen— led by Ned—running up the corridor toward them.

"Oh, no," Lance whispered.

In a matter of seconds Lance had been hand-cuffed and yanked to his feet. Nancy kept the gun on him the whole time. Then she turned and handed it to one of the officers. "You may want to hang on to this," she said.

"Yes, maybe so," the officer agreed, smiling.

The policeman holding Lance jerked on his

arm. "Come on," he said. "We've got a nice place waiting for you. Not quite Saint-Tropez, though, I'm afraid."

"Bess!" Lance said as the officers started to lead him away. "I just want you to know. If things had been different—well, it would have been fun knowing you."

Bess smiled bleakly. "Strange, Lance, but that doesn't make me feel too good."

Lance turned to Nancy. "You're a good detective. I wish I had killed you though."

"Well, it doesn't look as though you'll get another chance, does it?" Nancy answered.

The three girls and Ned watched as the police led Lance out of the airport and into a patrol car.

"Well, that's the end of him," George said. "To tell you the truth, I'm glad this case is over. It was a little too close for me."

"Yes, and I almost blew the whole thing," Bess said. "You both could have been killed, and it would have been all my fault! I feel awful. This is the worst job I've ever done."

"Don't feel bad, Bess," Nancy said. "We all let our emotions rule our minds from time to time."

"You don't," Ned muttered beside her.

Nancy threw him an apologetic look. "We'll talk later," she whispered. "Anyway, Bess," she went on matter-of-factly, "it all worked out.

That's what's important. Come on, let's get out of here."

The four of them walked out of the airport terminal and onto the sidewalk.

"The thing is," Bess said wistfully, "he seemed like such a nice guy."

"Nice, maybe, but not too smart," George said.

"I know," Nancy agreed. "How did he think he was going to get through airport security with that gun?"

"Oh, he had that all worked out," Bess said. "He told me about it on the way to the airport. I guess he was just so sure he had the perfect plan that he just had to tell somebody."

"Well, tell *us*," said George. "How'd he plan to beat the security checks?"

"It wasn't that brilliant, actually. He was just going to ditch the gun before he went through the metal detector," Bess said.

The four friends were outside then, and the morning sun was well up in the sky. It suddenly occurred to Nancy that she couldn't remember the last time she had eaten.

"Hey, let's celebrate the closing of this case with some waffles for breakfast," Nancy said. "I've really worked up an appetite."

"Sounds great to me," George agreed.

Bess frowned and turned away. "I don't know," she said softly. "I really don't deserve to be a part of this celebration. Why don't you go on without me?"

Nancy, Ned, and George looked at one another in concern. Nancy was sure they were all thinking the same thing: if Bess was turning down food, she must be even more upset than she sounded.

"We're certainly *not* going on without you," Nancy said.

"You're being crazy," George agreed, poking Bess in the arm. "We've humored you all we're going to. Besides, you know you love waffles. If you're going to pass up those warm, buttery goodies that melt in your mouth, you deserve to be left alone." She grabbed Bess by the shirt-sleeve. "Now come on."

A broad grin spread across Bess's face. "Well—" she said. "Maybe just one." She thought for a second. "And some bacon. And maybe some orange juice. Oh, and of course, a cup of coffee."

They were all grinning by then. They decided to let the police pick up the motorcycle, and they all climbed into Bess's car.

"We're going to eat those waffles. But tomorrow we're going to have to go on a diet," Nancy said, looking at Bess and trying to hold in her giggles. "We really need to lose about five pounds."

"How did you know?" Bess asked innocently.

They were all laughing hysterically as they drove off.

Breakfast was over. Bess had dropped Nancy and Ned off at Nancy's house, and they were sitting on the front porch together—the same porch where they'd spent a happy time together just a few weeks before.

Now, though, Nancy wasn't feeling nearly so happy. Ned had seemed quiet at the restaurant, and she wasn't quite sure what to say about the past few days.

It was Ned who finally broke the silence. "So," he said, "what's going to happen to Hal?"

Nancy sighed. "I don't know. He's really had a pretty rough time. I'm not saying he handled things the right way, but I realize now that it's not all his fault. It must have been awful having a guardian like Lance.

"Anyway," she went on, "I'll call my father tonight and tell him all about this. I think Hal's going to need a lawyer—especially now that he doesn't have a guardian anymore. Maybe my dad can take the case."

"And speaking of calling people—" Ned began.

Nancy looked down. "Oh, Ned, I've been feeling so terrible! I didn't want to tell you about this—and I didn't want to keep it a secret—and I guess I just made a mess of everything."

"Why didn't you want to tell me about the case?" Ned asked, his voice carefully neutral.

"I told myself it was because you had to write your paper. But, Ned, it was really because I didn't want another big discussion about my job."

"That's what Bess thought. She filled me in on everything while we waited outside that apartment. And I have to admit that at first I was pretty mad that you'd kept this a secret."

"I was afraid of that," Nancy said softly. "But I was also afraid you'd want me to drop the case."

"Well, I might have," Ned answered. "But when I got to the airport and saw you standing over Lance with that gun, I realized you can handle pretty much anything that comes your way. I decided it would have been awfully patronizing of me to tell you to stay away from the dangerous cases.

"And you know what?" he said, taking her hand in his. "I think that we should both stop worrying about what I think of your job and just let you do it. Let's try anyway."

"Oh, Ned!" Nancy felt light-headed with

relief. She threw her arms around his neck. "That would be great," she said. "And you know what? I think that right now we should both stop talking about my job. Remember how I said we'd have to come up with a way to celebrate the end of your paper over the phone? Well, there are probably a lot more ways to do it in person, wouldn't you say?"

Ned smiled and kissed her gently. "I can think of a few," he said.

Nancy's next case:

An airline trainee dies under suspicious circumstances—and a friend asks Nancy Drew to investigate. Is Jennifer Bishop right? Was Rod Fullerton
murdered?

Nancy is determined to find out, with a two-prong
plan of attack. She'll be out in the open, investigating, while Bess goes undercover as a flight attendant.

Can Nancy survive flying the deadly skies? Find out
in *WINGS OF FEAR,* Case #13 in The Nancy Drew
Files.

If you tune in to *Miami Vice* and *Moonlighting*, rock to MTV, and want to be in on what's happening *next*—read...

Pink Flamingos™

CREATED BY JOHN SANSEVERE &
CAROL Q. SANSEVERE

ILLUSTRATED BY WILLIAM RIESER

It's a hot new idea with a hot new look—a graphic novel with art so sophisticated it bursts off the page in an explosion of visual energy. The story is a sensational mix of friendship, love, danger, and commitment. And it's all done with a tilt toward fashion, style, and attitude.

PINK FLAMINGOS

They're five beautiful young women on the edge of love and danger

LANA—blond, 17, and a model. Her beauty and innocence can't protect her from a fatal attraction to the wrong men.

CARLA—17, fronts a rock band with a latino/funk sound. Assertive and charming, she's a sucker for a friend in need.

JODY—18 and totally at odds with her wealthy social background. She's hard to love, too easy to hurt.

JACKIE—18, beautiful, ambitious, and smart. An intern at WKTV Palm Beach, she can make things happen.

AMBER—18 and a member of a motorcycle gang. A tawny-maned beauty from the wrong side of the tracks, she's got spunk and style.

(Continued on following page)

BOOK ONE: BRING DOWN THE NIGHT

It started with a fur coat. Lana thought it was a gift, but there were strings attached, and they led straight to a man who wouldn't take no for an answer. The situation is beyond her charm, and she's scared. Enter the Pink Flamingos. Together they confront the man, uncovering the dark side that lurks beneath the elegant surface of Palm Beach—and blow the lid off a million-dollar scam.

Pink Flamingos

GET IT...
AT YOUR LOCAL BOOKSTORE

A Simon & Schuster Graphic Novel

Pink Flamingos is a trademark of Angel Entertainment, Inc.

- -

Simon & Schuster, Mail Order Dept. PFN
200 Old Tappan Rd., Old Tappan, NJ 07675

_____ Book One: **BRING DOWN THE NIGHT** 0-671-63149-7
8½ x 11, full color, $6.95

Please send me the book I have checked above. I am enclosing $_____ (Please add $1.00 to cover postage and handling for each order. NYS and NYC residents please add appropriate sales tax.) Send check or money order—no cash or COD's please. Allow up to six weeks for delivery. For purchases over $10.00 you may use VISA; card number expiration date and customer signature must be included.

NAME _____

ADDRESS _____

CITY _____ STATE / ZIP _____

VISA CARD NO. _____ EXP. DATE _____

SIGNATURE _____

154

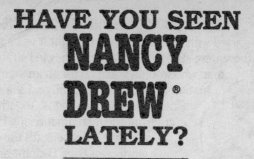